Reviews for OUTSIDER (2012)

"*Outsider* by W. Freedreamer Tinkanesh, provides a fascinating ride through the minds of multiple abstract characters, and their interactions with one another." Elyse Draper, author of the *Freewill* trilogy

"It is as if Nancy A. Collins, Anne Rice, Poppy Z. Brite and Bram Stoker all got together to create a vampire for the punk era." Rick Powell, author of *A Vault of Whispers*

Review for TALES FOR THE 21ˢᵗ CENTURY (volume 1, 2014)

"For me this book was a wonderful revisiting of some of my favorite stories by W. Freedreamer Tinkanesh. Many of these stories I'd read before, when they appeared either as stand-alone stories or as part of some other collections.

If you have never read any of this author's work before, this is the volume to start with." Hydra M. Star, owner of *Infernal Ink Books*

TALES FOR THE 21st CENTURY
Volume 2
by
W. Freedreamer Tinkanesh

Tales for the 21st Century volume 2
Copyright © 2019 W. Freedreamer Tinkanesh

ISBN: 9781081084882

Cover Design
by W. Freedreamer Tinkanesh

..*.*.*

..*.*.*

DEDICATION

To the memory of my friend Jennifer L. Miller (February 13, 1978 – March 31, 2019) fellow writer, editor and mastermind of the Ladies and Gentlemen (of Horror and of Fantasy) anthologies

And to the memory of my best friend Jane Timm Baxter (April 16, 1976 – April 12, 2019) fellow writer, artist and multi-talented human being

Each life you touched is now richer

May your spirits fly free and soar high, my friends, you are loved and forever remembered

Contents

Dedication   5
Table of Contents   7
Grateful Thanx   8
Foreword   9
Central Library Calling   13
The Lost Librarian   31
In the Shadow of Central Library   55
The Last One Left Travelling   75
Children of the Sand   93
Alive or Dead   107
Michaela   113
The Blood of an Enemy   119
Remembering Jennifer L. Miller   131
Remembering Jane Timm Baxter   133
About the Author   135

GRATEFUL THANX to

Jane Timm Baxter,
Elyse Draper,
Jennifer L. Miller,
SW Fairbrother,
Zhana,
Elizabeth Watasin,
librarians and libraries,
and those who believe (you know who you are).

Foreword

Welcome to the worlds and mind of W. Freedreamer Tinkanesh. Collections, such as this, are a gift from the writer to their readers; a chance to experience the broad strokes of an author's imagination, through obscure landscapes, while holding the hands of new characters with each new story. W's take on life, society, nature, and love is always a unique and brilliant ride... Oh, how I envy the journey you are going to take, when your imaginings mingle with the vision shared in these narratives.

In all the years I have known this gifted artist, through music, paint, photographs and words, W has taken me to meet the queer, the broken, the hardened, and the misunderstood. I have loved them all, in graveyards where they chose to lay with their fallen loves to the magically anthropomorphic fighters, who possess a subtle fragility. The scenery is cast from cathedrals built within the sprawling outstretched canopies of nature's grace, the dark contrast of humanity's grief cut stunningly through cemetery, mausoleum, and marble, and the voices who whisper from dusty pages to those who care for them the most. There is no telling what you will find as you read along the warped and winding road; however, you will find pieces of yourself in the wisps of breathtaking weirdness along the way.

Please, enjoy the journey, as I always have,

Elyse Draper

CENTRAL LIBRARY CALLING
*(edited by Jennifer L. Miller and previously published in the
Ladies and Gentlemen of Horror 2017)*

THE LOST LIBRARIAN
(edited by Zhana)

IN THE SHADOW OF CENTRAL LIBRARY
(edited by Zhana)

CENTRAL LIBRARY CALLING

-I-

Mair stretched her back at her desk and sighed. Her dark brown eyes, barely darker than her skin, found the fading sunlight fighting its way into the library through a grimy skylight. It was almost closing time. El, on duty at the loan desk in the public room downstairs, would announce so any minute now. Mair pushed her glasses up to her hairline and rubbed her eyes, grateful that the religious zealot hadn't come into Central Library to make a scene on the longest day of the week.

"Okay," she mumbled to herself. "Let's see......." She focused her attention on the aging computer that had just gone into sleep mode in front of her and gently, but firmly, pressed the space bar. The machine slowly wheezed back to life. The senior librarian clicked the 'Fines' folder open and grimaced. Spring was in sight, the winds were gathering, the tuned spires of every church in Prahak were getting ready to 'sing', and the one leprechaun in Spider District had a book overdue by two weeks.

"Ray!" She called out to her junior colleague on the other side of the long room, her voice gently echoing. "It's your turn to retrieve overdue items tonight. I email you the details."

The grey-eyed womon looked up from her own computer, blinked like an owl and smiled. "Send over!" Her voice echoing, too, in their sparsely furnished office.

Mair pressed the 'Send' key. "Be wary. It's the leprechaun. Do not bargain with him. Stick to protocol. He is a tricky little bugger, and he's got the gift of the gab. Rainbow or not, stick, to, protocol."

The pony-tailed womon nodded and started reading the details now showing on her monitor. "Connor O'Connor, Pretik Alley 44." While this leprechaun was notorious at the Central Library, it was the first time in her five years of library service that she would deal with him.

Ray stood up after switching her computer off and stretched up and out her five feet and seven inches. Today, like most days, she was wearing black trainers, tan trousers, a simple white shirt and a grey waistcoat. A standard outfit for most librarians that fitted her thin-ish frame perfectly. She grabbed her librarian ID card and stuck it into a back pocket. She tapped the front pockets of her trousers and felt a set of keys. Satisfied, she declared, "I'm off."

"Good luck!" Mair replied.

* * * *

Every spring, Connor O'Connor had trouble treating deadlines with care and respect, and was at his grumpiest, like any respectable leprechaun in the Prahak Shehrar Republic. People wanting to hang on to their sanity and equilibrium would postpone any dealing with the Irish creatures until after the first High Winds of the year. Except the librarians. Librarians were a rare breed, sworn in to protect books, libraries and their traditions. They worked long hours for a low pay and rooming within the walls of their workplace. Being a librarian was a sacred calling that no one else could understand, not even the volunteers who gave a few precious hours of their time every week for the love of reading.

Pretik Alley was a previously merchant artery breathing west of the Viliver River, the west confluent of the Vlativer River, the main body of water in the country that split Prahak into two geographical halves.

Number 44 was the most affluent house, quietly baroque, at the bottom of the alley. Ray's trainers hitting the cobblestones barely echoed. She suspected half the houses stood empty and slowly crumbling within.

She pulled the bell chain at the shiny and wide wooden door, library ID card at the ready, and listened to the chime ricocheting inside. Daylight was retreating out of the city, giving in to the ominous presence of evening. Heavy footfalls and the regular click of a walking stick crowded the silence.

"Who is it?" A grumbling resonated out of an entry phone Ray hadn't noticed yet.

"Central Library calling." She answered with the official greeting. Looking at the entry phone, she positioned her ID card for the eye of the camera.

Angry mumblings followed. The door suddenly opened, slamming against a wall, and Connor O'Connor stood in front of the junior librarian, as tall as one possibly could when only five feet of height. And as leprechauns go, he was tall. "What do you want?" It was more an irate shout than a friendly query.

"I am here representing Central library of Spider District from the City of Prahak, regarding item number 3465, a book entitled 'Rare Coffees of Ecuador'. It is currently two weeks overdue and incurs a fine of seven billars."

She couldn't help but stare at Connor O'Connor. It was one thing to look at pictures of leprechauns in a book, and another to see one in wizened flesh and red jacket, with seven rows of seven buttons on each row, under a worn-out leather apron. The red-buckled boots were a shiny black and the breeches were as red as the jacket.

"I wear red, so what!" The angry shout distorted his bearded features. "As a librarian, you should know about it!" True, the green clothes were actually worn by younger leprechauns;

Connor O'Connor was so old, no one knew the age of the legendary shoemaker. "What do you want?" He shouted impatiently.

She patiently and politely repeated the traditional request. Library costumers were to be treated with respect at all times, no matter how rude their behaviour.

"Seven billars? What kind of a joke is that! Go away before I beat you up with my shillelagh!" His right hand reached for the wide knob of the knotty stick leaning against the wall by the entryway and froze, resting on the polished blackthorn wood. His face was fixed in almost terror. Eventually, after Ray's eyebrows rose with surprise, he sighed, anger gone out of his voice. "You've got a Ray-Nor......."

She turned to her left and stared in amazement at the monkey-like creature standing two steps behind her. She noticed the black, coarse fur, the razor-sharp teeth when it smiled dangerously, and the strong shoulder muscles. It looked like a spider monkey, but taller. The long prehensile tail was gently swaying like a slow metronome.

"I'll go and get the book," Connor said behind her with apprehension colouring his voice.

Suddenly the Ray-Nor jumped with feline speed. Its clawed hands and hand-like feet took hold of the sides of the doorway and the door itself, preventing the leprechaun to lock himself in. The Ray-Nor hissed. And barked like a furious dog. The shillelagh clattered onto the wooden floor.

The librarian felt in awe.

The leprechaun looked miserable. "Okay, okay." His voice sounded subdued. "I'll be right back. I promise." He walked away without picking up the walking stick. His shoulders stooped, he stepped into a room opening on the side of the long corridor tunnelling into the depths of his house. Two short minutes later he

16

was back and the Ray-Nor let him stand on the threshold. "Here." He handed a hardback book to Ray and started opening a pouch previously hidden under his leather apron.

A low growl rumbled up and out of the Ray-Nor's throat. The razor-sharp teeth inched closer to the leprechaun's face.

Connor froze. His fingers dropped the pouch. He sighed. True to legend, the Ray-Nor couldn't be fooled with a cheap trick of dry leaves. "How much did you say?" He mumbled to Ray, his eyes avoiding hers.

"Seven billars, please."

He pulled a billfold out of a back pocket, slowly counted seven notes and handed them over to the librarian with reluctant hands. The Ray-Nor let go of the doorway and retreated to the pavement.

"Central Library thanks you and looks forward to your next visit." The door slammed closed in Ray's face before the end of the traditional greeting. The Ray-Nor's emerald green eyes met her grey ones, looking as human as hers.

The creature jumped away and disappeared into the darkening evening, leaving her standing with a book in one hand and seven billars in the other. She heard the wolf howl of Spider Church, quickly followed by the eagle cry of Kohoph Church and more echoing sounds. It was officially night-time.

"I've got a Ray-Nor! I've got a Ray-Nor!" The excited Ray bounced into the private shared quarters of the librarians, in the attic of the library.

Mair looked up from a newspaper she was reading at the communal table. "A Ray-Nor?" She smiled. In the 20 years she had worked at the Prahak Central Library, it was the first of these semi-mythical creatures attaching itself to a librarian from Spider District.

"A Ray-Nor?" El and her long, dark and coppery brown hair came out of the small kitchen where she had just finished preparing their dinner. A kabosha soup with bannock on the side. Well, kabosha squashes were not available in Shehrar; El had used a butternut squash forgotten at the back of the larder and surprisingly still edible. It was her turn to cook this week. At this time of the year, she felt the need to counteract the High Winds with the comforting food she had been brought up with in North America. Her grey eyes had a metallic tinge darker than Ray's. As most evenings, she was wearing blue, bagging gym trousers, as old as they were comfortable.

"Yes!" Enthusiasm sounded loud and clear in Ray's voice.

"Tell us!" Mair's tone was as eager as El's facial expression. The first Ray-Nor in ten years.......

Ray started telling her story, first retelling the anger of the Leprechaun in his red outfit, and his sudden fear at the sight of the Ray-Nor. She described the claws, the eyes, the tail, the monkey-like fur.

"It looked like a monkey? What kind of monkey?" Mair wanted to know.

Ray hesitated, recalling in her mind's eye the facial features of the creature, the strange hint of longing in its shiny green eyes. "It was a tall version of a spider monkey."

Later that night, searching for sleep and dreams in her narrow bed, Ray remembered her friend Nor, a green-eyed junior librarian from the Kohoph District. Not the first librarian to disappear, she had been missing for 13 months. The last time they had seen each other, they had been to a semi-legal drag king club on a Saturday night. Nor's eyes were as green as the shiniest emeralds. She was quiet and always keen on discovering new knowledge. These qualities had immediately attracted Ray at their first meeting during an inter-district library conference. Despite her average height, she stood out to Ray's attention. Maybe it was the black clothes. Or the sudden smile when Ray accosted her and introduced herself. The connection had been instant, and while librarians' conversations tended to gravitate around the Dewey System, theirs expended very quickly to life, politics, drag king culture and beyond.

Politics were generally accursed as they had tightened budgets all over the Prahak Shehrar Republic (Shehrar for short). While libraries had been mostly kept (people's uproar didn't give the corrupt government many options), the number of junior librarians had been reduced. Libraries were run by a senior librarian working with two junior librarians and as many volunteers as would join.

Ray would have wanted more out of her friendship with Nor, she was sure her feelings were reciprocated, but her friend disappeared within days of their visit to the drag king club. Ray still felt fascination for Nor's knowledge of drag king history in Shehrar and beyond.

At last, when the old Velidar Church struck 3 am on Old Town Square, the junior librarian fell asleep, holding onto something that hadn't been.

-II-

"Yes, Kolish, what can I do for you?" El politely greeted the middle-aged man whose regularly shaved head was shining as if polished with bee wax and as much as the 15-cm-long cross he proudly carried hanging from his neck.

A religious zealot, the man was a regular at the Central Library and was known to complain more often than not. He came to the venerable building twice a week, regardless of the days, and buried himself in the Religions section, reverently consulting the manuscripts and endlessly comparing religions. Today, his request was unusually quiet, the approach of the High Winds affecting his demeanour. "Would you have a pencil?" He deposited a single coin on the junior librarian's desk. El handed over the purchased item. "Thank you." His eyes and mind were already elsewhere as he absentmindedly accepted the pencil.

After Kolish turned his back and walked away, El let out a silent sigh of relief. Today could still be a good day.

"Is it true?" A womon with silver-threaded black hair and with skin almost as dark as Mair's was now standing in front of El. There was a huge smile on her face and trepidation coloured her voice. "Ray has a Ray-Nor?"

El smiled back at Zekia. "Yes, it is true." The word had circulated fast.

"How exciting! Tell her that if she wants to know more about this rare creature, I'll be happy to help. I did some research about Ray-Nors a few years back. They're only mentioned in two volumes, and actually very little is known about them. Of course, if she is inclined to share, I'd love to hear the details."

"I'll let her know."

An authority in the cultural past and oddities of Prahak, Zekia was an eccentric scholar who lectured in History at Prahak High University. Patient and mild-mannered, she was liked by every librarian and volunteer, and almost everyone whose path entangled with hers.

El got up and walked away from her desk with Zekia matching her stride. They went into an adjacent room where the librarian unlocked a cabinet with a key from the bunch hooked to one of her belt loops. The eccentric scholar was currently studying manuscripts from the 19th century. The only copies known to exist were kept away from most people and only a few scholars were allowed access to them. Zekia was specifically searching for mentions of monsters. She felt like a new outbreak was close and wondered how far back in time she could find them. She had discovered an easy pattern through Prahak's time line: every time a Ray-Nor had appeared, as the first High Winds were building up, monsters had followed in its steps.

* * * *

"I know you'd like to talk with Zekia," Mair was telling Ray later that day, "but, since you have a Ray-Nor, you are now the best librarian to retrieve overdue items."

Ray smiled good-naturedly. "Okay." She cocked her head to one side. "Who is today's delinquent."

Mair grimaced.

"What?"

"It's Nikuos the vampire…….."

Ray's face froze on her smile while the single name echoed menacingly.

"A good thing you've got a Ray-Nor."

The what-if question stayed unspoken. Everyone preferred to think that the Ray-Nor would be there every time Ray needed backup, every time without failing.

"Okay……." Ray said, elongating the second syllable. She took a deep and slow breath.

"Do not step inside his house. Always stay where you can be seen by passers-by. Refuse every alternative he might suggest. Understood?"

"Yes," the junior librarian answered, her face now a study of seriousness. "Understood." If the Ray-Nor had been a god, she would have fervently prayed to it to insure its presence. However, the Ray-Nor was not a god, and, like El and Mair, Ray was an atheist.

* * * *

The vampire's house was a gothic affair that had seen better days.
Nikuos himself was not as dashing a socialite as he had been. He
still kept a ghoul for the menial tasks required within the quiet
walls of his home. The ghoul was a decrepit creature with a twisted
spine who had once been a man and was now a crawling servant
falling on his knees at a mere shout from his master. Like many
creatures in Prahak, the vampire couldn't wait for the first High
Winds to hit and be gone. The ghoul opened the door at the
librarian's pulling of the bell chain and before she could say a
word, a voice, deep and angry, resonated within the house. "Who is
it?"

"It's dinner!" The ghoul answered with glee distorting his
facial features into a horrid grimace.

"What are you waiting for? Bring it in!"

The ghoul extended a greedy arm, but before he could grab
the retreating Ray, a clawed hand locked itself around his grimy
sleeve.

"Guerande! I am hungry!" The angry voice burst with
impatience.

"Ahh! Master!" The ghoul cried out in fear, his yellow eyes
staring into emerald eyes.

"What?" Like anger hammering nails into a skull.

"A Ray-Nor!" The ghoul's feet gave way and he lets
himself fall to the stone floor of the entryway, the mythical creature
holding him up by the arm. He whimpered.

Slow, heavy footsteps echoed through the long and dark
corridor. Ray stared at the approaching shadow taking shape. The
Ray-Nor had let go of the ghoul, now curled up into a pathetic ball

22

against a wall, and it, too, was watching the vampire nearing their dramatic group.

Ray was not sure what to do. She hesitated and, prodded by training, decided to stick to her pre-ordered script. With a slight tremble in her voice, she recited, "Central Library calling." The vampire kept his approach slow and steady, his features unreadable in the dim light. Ray went on, her voice shaking. "I am here representing Central Library of Spider District from the City of Prahak, regarding item number 6156, a book entitled 'The Countess Bathory's Life and Times'. It is currently two weeks overdue and incurs a fine of seven billars."

The Ray-Nor hissed at the vampire.

Without the creature's presence, Ray's speech would have dissolved into incomprehensible sounds and she would have run for her life, run all throughout the night to the point where the sun rises.

The vampire was impressive, despite the blood stains on his creased waistcoat. As handsome as the mythical dark and tall stranger, he smiled at the librarian, revealing canines and incisors, sharp as a sabre-tooth's gnashers, shiny and pearly-white. His eyes were dazzling and icy blue under the dark curls gracing his pale forehead.

Ray could feel the vampiric magnetism working on her willpower. She wondered if –and hoped that– the Ray-Nor was immune to supernatural charm.

Arms open wide to accentuate the welcoming tone of his voice, the vampire said, "Forgive my servant's impudence!" He oozed malevolent power.

The Ray-Nor hissed.

Ray felt lost and helpless.

"So, it is true," the vampire said with false awe, his eyes studying the mythical creature, and carefully keeping a safe distance between them. "There is a Ray-Nor in Spider District." His eyes moved to Ray's eyes. His voice smooth, he continued. "And you are the lucky librarian. Please, come in. My useless servant will prepare some tea, or whatever you wish to drink. It would be such a pleasure to converse with you."

Ray felt the magnetic pull tugging at her. She felt her muscles tense to step in, but, as she started lifting a foot, the Ray-Nor growled and positioned itself squarely in the doorway.

The vampire's face tensed. "Your Ray-Nor is welcome, too, of course."

The Ray-Nor tensed its muscles, ready to attack. He hissed dangerous promises.

The vampire's smile faltered.

Ray remembered mair's words. *Do not step inside his house. Always stay where you can be seen by passers-by. Refuse every alternative he might suggest.* She felt herself taking one step forward. The back of the Ray-Nor put a solid stop to her advance. Her voice was tainted with fear; her words were more mumbling than proud introduction. "I am here representing Central Library of Spider District from the City of Prahak, regarding item 6156, a book entitled 'The Countess Bathory's Life and Times'. It is currently two weeks overdue–"

"If this is the way you want to play it." The smile disappeared from the vampire's face and his eyes darkened. He roared but, before his hand could punch the Ray-Nor out of the way and grab Ray by her pony tail, a clawed hand slashed across his face and his arm leaving a bloody trail.

The ghoul scrambled out of the way.

The Ray-Nor bodily shoved the librarian to the side.

The vampire hurled himself forward.

The Ray-Nor bit the pristine side of his face.

The last sun rays pushed Nikuos back into his house. Hands cradling his head, he retreated silently.

The Ray-Nor stood motionless, a lip curl decorating its face.

The vampire turned around, the tip of his booted foot violently connecting with the ghoul's ribcage. "Guerande!" Anger roared in his voice. "You heard the librarian! Get the bloody book and some damn coins!"

* * * *

"Yes," Zekia said. "While it is not known if it is the same Ray-Nor returning or a new one appearing, it is generally followed by an outbreak of monsters. Especially at this time of the year."

It was evening time. Library users and volunteers had left and gone home, or wherever their lifestyle took them. Ray, Mair, El and Zekia were sitting at a round table in the archives room where the scholar frequently read, compared and analyzed. Every face was serious and attentive.

After a silence, Zekia resumed. "There is one sketch portraying a Ray-Nor, and a physical description. There is a record of Ray-Nor sightings. But no one can say if it is male, female, or genderless. Of course, there are many speculations, but nothing logical, let alone definitive. Why would its appearance be followed by an outbreak of monsters is also opened to speculations."

"What about the monsters?" Mair queried. "No sighting has been reported."

"Yet."

"What kind of monsters should we expect?" El asked.

"They are different every time. Twenty-seven years ago, there was a major heat wave in Prahak. The monsters were huge and reptilian. Fifteen years prior to them, they were insect-like creatures of humongous scale. In 1964, they were subterranean and mostly lived in the sewage. Crocodiles paled in comparison. I have recently studied 19th century manuscripts and I believed I found the first ever instance in 1856. The descriptions are reminiscent of pterodactyls. Flying reptiles from the Jurassic and Cretaceous periods. There is no pattern time-wise. However, before the monsters and before the Ray-Nor, there is one preceding event."

The librarians looked at the scholar, expectation tensing muscles on each face.

"I have noticed that at least prior to this year, prior to 1987, 1972, 1964 and 1948, someone disappeared the year before. A librarian."

Silence greeted the revelation. At last, Ray whispered, "Nor......."

* * * *

They came from the sky, at night, humming along the song of the first High Winds as they played with the tuned spires of every church in Prahak. They preyed on human beings and feasted on the victims' entrails. Fearful of the twilight, people, human and otherwise, locked their doors before the first touch of the night. Even vampires were feeling fretful. Werewolves stared silently at the moon. Only a librarian protected by a Ray-Nor was believed to be safe under the stars, while the spires refined their tuning with almost hysterical overtones.

-III-

Ray had retrieved three library books that evening, without incidents as every culprit was a human with a harassed look. As a consequence, she had not seen the Ray-Nor and its soulful eyes.

She wondered if it was watching from the rooftops. Night had fallen and the streets were uncannily quiet in the lull of the High Winds. People were afraid. The eccentric scholar had told the librarians it was probably the worst outbreak of monsters experienced in the history of Prahak. Newspapers had reported several dozen people dead or missing in the past fortnight, including a werewolf and the unsavoury ghoul Ray had the unpleasantness of encountering recently. The flying monsters attacked in pairs and always got their prey. The rare witnesses still alive to tell the tale –and holding onto their sanity by a thin thread of spider silk– couldn't agree on the creatures' appearance. One said bats, another said birds, a third one –in an advance state of alcoholic torpor– said gargoyles. The only exaggerated detail agreed upon was the gigantic size.

Lampposts were casting yellow light on the dirty pavement and the air felt still and expectant. Ray looked up at the dark sky. Stars were hidden by clouds. She wondered what Prahak looked like when seen from outer space.

She felt the air caress her face as lightly as a feather. She looked up to a roof covering a three-storey house and guessed the alert presence of the Ray-Nor. She looked around her. The air was moving gently and lazily. Like the ocean waves under the moon, or the slow wings of a bird…….

Ray heard the caw of the strange creature at the same time as the Ray-Nor landed on top of it. It looked like a giant bat with dark feathery wings. Ray's protector snapped the creature's neck with one swift move, freezing the gaping jaws in a savage rictus. The Ray-Nor jumped off and the monster grotesquely fell to the ground. Angry cawing erupted from the sky. Ray started to run with a death grip on the three library books. She was two corners away from the Central Library. She had one Ray-Nor, but the purported pair of flying creatures sounded like a huge mob of monsters in the sky, their cries bouncing off the walls like a cacophony of bats startled in their cave.

The Ray-Nor was efficient. Two giant bats cracked their heads against each other.

Ray made it round the last corner. A feathery wing slapped her in the face. She fell to the ground and rolled, dropping the books. She saw the Ray-Nor fiercely piercing two hearts with bloody claws. Monsters covered it. The world exploded in Ray's head.

* * * *

Ray closed her eyes as soon as she opened them. The ceiling light above her was blinding. When she heard a jingling of chains, she carefully, and only slightly, lifted her eyelids, her eyes looking away from the naked light bulb hanging down from a ceiling higher than she had first thought. Her eyesight slowly focused on the Ray-Nor. It was chained to a white wall. Its open emerald eye latched onto her grey ones. The other one hid behind swollen eyelids.

"Ah, you are awake." A male voice on her left.

She tried to move. Her wrists, ankles, waist and neck were strapped to a bed. Or a table. She wasn't sure which, but it felt solid and cold. She turned her head towards the left and saw a man comfortably sitting on a chair with armrests. His face looked familiar. Wasn't he a member of the government? A vague memory of a TV appearance wandered through her mind. Yes, a middle-ranking government official. His name was……. Revek. His family was of merchant wealth and known for their meddling with politics for a few centuries. His wrinkles and sparse white hair showed age; the shadows under his eyes showed exhaustion. His eyes and smile had hints of cruelty.

He chuckled. "I never thought this little monster of mine would attach itself to a librarian named Ray." He laughed harder.

Ray felt too sluggish to do more than stare. What was he on about? Her eyes moved back to the Ray-Nor, who was fighting its chains.

He mused, "Mix the genes of an ateles with a homo bibliothecarius." He stopped and added as an afterthought, "a spider monkey and a librarian." His smile widened. "This is the genetic recipe for a Ray-Nor. Why do people call it a Ray-Nor? I have no idea. I call it homo ateles. This Ray-Nor chose you. Maybe it already knew you......."

Ray's sluggish brain was refusing an interpretation.

"Oh, yes, this Ray-Nor was your friend. I picked this librarian because she used to irritate the hell out of me." The tone of his voice was now hard as stone, almost a mumble. "Refusing to be feminine, never smiling, barely polite. Bloody librarians." His facial features distorted into a hateful grimace.

Ray didn't want to look at him. Her eyes focused on the one soft emerald eye again.

"Clever little monsters, these Ray-Nors. They always manage to escape. Their propensity to protect librarians must be due to their genes. I've been trying to get this detail out of their makeup."

Ray remembered Nor's eyes. The same pure emerald green.

"The other monsters. Ha! I love the way they terrorize Prahak. Beside being entertaining, they are easy to control."

He was waiting for her to speak, but she only gave him silence.

"And why would I kidnap another librarian so soon? I have plans for you. I considered the genes of a gorilla gorilla and a homo bibliothecarius. My ancestors never tried. But then, I thought....." He was pompously warming up to his subject. "Homo ateles and homo bibliothecarius. I wonder what the result would be. Would this new monster protect a librarian, or kill them? At the very least, I'd do this country a great service and I would do myself a favour: one less librarian to piss me off." There was such hatred in his voice that Ray would have stepped back if she hadn't been tightly strapped to the cold table. "I watched the two of you, perverts. Ah, you wanted to be with her?" He burst out laughing. "I hope this 'threesome' doesn't feel too crowded!" His fingers shaped air quotes close to her face.

The Ray-Nor started fighting its chains again. The man stood up, still laughing, his cruel cackle echoing eerily against distant and immaculate walls, and walked out of the vast room.

THE LOST LIBRARIAN
(Sequel to 'Central Library Calling')

"For Sid, playing with monsters was the equivalent of playing
with genders."
W. Freedreamer Tinkanesh (in 'Outsider')

-I-

The longest day of the week at the library was almost over. El
would announce so in the public room downstairs any minute now.
She would make sure every reader exited the premises and then she
would lock the tall double door gracing the entrance with finely
carved, solid oak wood. She would set the alarm system –
teenagers had been known to crash into the baroque building for
parties with alcohol and the odd illegal substance. The intrusion of
a police squad didn't discourage them from returning to their
debauchery a few months later. The young delinquents had never
found the hidden staircase that took librarians to their private
sanctum.

In the kitchen, El would pick up some shredded chicken she
had left to thaw and take it to the roof. There a cat was waiting
behind a chimney pot. It was bigger than a Main Coon, even bigger
than a Norwegian Forest cat, and while retaining the general frame
of the cold-climate feline, its outward appearance was of a Siamese
cat with almost human grey eyes. The cautious cat would let El

watch the ritual dinner while a very normal murder of hopeful crows was on watchful attendance for leftovers. The mysterious cat would rarely leave any scrap. After a last mouthful, it would look at the librarian, squarely meeting her gaze for a few seconds, and would depart for destination unknown.

Meanwhile, Mair, in the long room used as office by the librarians, pushed her glasses up to the bridge of her nose, and clicked open the 'Fines' folder in the aging computer. After five seconds that felt like five minutes, her dark brown eyes, barely darker than her skin, scanned the short list of potential culprits. Spring was in the air, winds were about to gather, and tuned spires of every church in the city of Prahak were bracing themselves for 'singing'. It was the night before full moon and a werewolf local to Spider District had a book overdue by two weeks.

She sighed. She missed Ray and she missed Ray's Ray-Nor. Ray had gone missing the previous spring, when an outbreak of monsters had plagued the capital of the Prahak Shehrar Republic. The flying monsters had rampaged the sky, dive-bombed into the streets, foraging for lives for a fortnight, before disappearing the same night the junior librarian had failed to return from a collection round despite her protective Ray-Nor.

Since then a few harmless creatures had appeared here and there. These included the mysterious feline fed by El, and a canine that was as much a dog as a wallaby and who had adopted one of the librarian volunteers, a bright young womon with a rare passion for books and animals.

Ray had not been replaced yet, partly because Mair and El couldn't imagine anyone else sharing the library attic with them, partly because governmental administration was deserving of its reputation for extreme slowness. A snail was more efficient in comparison.

The werewolf, named Antonia Guergov, was holding on to a copy of Mary Shelley's 'Frankenstein'. While this library user had never been any trouble for the Central Library, the year was getting to that time where every non-human customer was turning restless and unpredictable. Librarians didn't care about their customers' species. However, Nikuos the vampire and his new ghoul associate had been banned from Central Library after Nikuos's attempt to feed on Ray the previous spring. Ray had been lucky. On that occasion.

Mair grimaced. It was her turn to collect fines. She read the address, stood up and stretched, her eyes catching the dim light valiantly breaking through a skylight never cleaned. She opened a drawer from her desk, grabbed a set of keys and her librarian ID, and with determination setting her jaw, set off to accomplish her evening duty. Librarians were a special breed. None would ever back out and let fear turn them into a coward. Werewolf or not, the library user was just a library user owing an overdue book and seven billars to Central Library.

* * * *

Antonia Guergov was of the fearful omega variety. While not an arrogant alpha, she was sensitive to the phases of the moon and her shiny golden eyes were studying the meal option standing on her doorstep and reciting a standard script regarding the item numbered 2857.

Mair noticed the fidgety fingers and the upcoming sharpness of the teeth, but she was determined to stand her ground.

Antonia was torn between obedience to laws, bylaws and library regulations, and the fierce influence of the nocturnal satellite. The working of her jaws was a reflex and a warning the senior librarian could not ignore. But when the werewolf's human face relaxed and amazement spread over its features, the librarian's eyes followed the shiny gaze and saw.......

It was as tall as a gorilla and of similar shape, but the strong and square shoulders were narrower and there was a tail slowly waving like a pendulum. Not a Ray-Nor as anyone would expect. Not a spider monkey with a fierce attitude. More like a peaceful gorilla with intelligent and sad eyes. Grey eyes, almost human.

Antonia Guergov's gentle voice broke the silence, "I'll be right back." She softly padded away on her bare furry feet, followed by the Ray-Nor's benevolent gaze.

"Thank you," she told Mair when she came back with the book and seven coins.

"You are welcome," Mair replied automatically. "Central Library thanks you and looks forward to your next visit."

"Good night." The werewolf in mostly human shape, her eyes staring at the unusual Ray-Nor, slowly closed her front door.

"Good night," Mair greeted back, and looked to her left for another gaze at the mysterious creature, but it had quietly disappeared.

* * * *

In his secret laboratory, a man with sparse white hair and shadows of exhaustion under his eyes was watching the scene on a computer screen. With disbelief. The creature would have killed him with bare hands and sharp teeth if given a chance. Its fury had even bent the bars of its cell, but not enough to get its muscled bulk through. Gorilla Bibliothecarius looked like a great success. The strength and the fury, the ravenous hate and the salivating need for predation. Librarians would soon be an extinct species!

But Revek, a middle-ranking government official, had never read books about gorillas or any other animals. It was way beneath his high scientific intellect.

-II-

"Hello, my name is Tarn. I believe you are expecting me tonight."

Mair looked up, surprised, and saw an arm extended for a handshake, a smiling face and engaging green eyes. "... Sorry?"

The smile faltered at Mair's serious face. "You haven't received a letter from the Ministry of Education? I've got mine here."

The tall womon with dark curls gently stroking her broad shoulders seemed to lose her confidence. She dropped her bulging backpack next to her equally bulging suitcase and started foraging in her raincoat pockets, then her trousers pockets, with growing agitation.

"I guess the administrative services failed again." Mair relaxed her face and smiled.

Tarn froze for a second and her left hand dove into the right inside pocket of her coat. She offered a folded and crumpled sheet of paper to Mair. The senior librarian stood up, accepted the letter and extended her right hand. Tarn grew a new smile, even if still a bit worried.

"I am Mair, senior librarian."

They shook hands, both with thoughts of concern. It was well known that librarians working together tended to develop strong bonds. Mair and El were still grieving for Ray. Tarn wasn't sure how welcome she was. Mair was thinking, *No, she is not getting Ray's room*. Fortunately, there was a spare room, dusty with disuse, that everyone had been ignoring for years. It would do.

It was 5.30 pm on Saturday and the library was quiet. El was due to relieve Mair at the main desk on the public floor any minute. The junior librarian was actually just a few steps away. And so was Zekia, the eccentric scholar. Mair looked from one to the other. Tarn followed her lead, recognizing El as a librarian because of the familiar style of clothing – waistcoat, white shirt and tan chino, and wondered who the other woman with silver-threaded black hair and skin almost as dark as Mair's could possibly be.

"Mair! Mair!" The woman was calling with excitement in her voice. "Have you heard? The new Ray-Nor was in Kohoph District yesterday evening!"

"A Ray-Nor?" Tarn exclaimed.

"In Kohoph?" El echoed, now standing by the desk.

The eccentric scholar, breathless, reached the desk and noticed Tarn. "Oh, sorry. Please, I can wait." She volunteered, restraining her excitement with difficulty. She saw the backpack and the suitcase. Her puzzlement mirrored El's.

"The Ray-Nor. In Kohoph." Mair whispered.

In the middle of the triangle, Tarn, one head taller than the three other wimin, cleared her throat and introduced herself, "Hi, I'm Tarn, the new junior librarian."

"Oh," Zekia said.

El stared, seemingly frozen.

"I know," Tarn told the established junior librarian with a worried tone. "The admin people failed to notify you of my appointment."

El relaxed and extended her right hand. "I'm El, junior librarian."

They shook hands, Tarn with relief, El with worry, green eyes meeting grey eyes.

36

"Of course," Mair declared, "if we had heard you were coming, we would have prepared a room for you. You'll have to forgive the state of the spare room."

"Of course."

El sighed silently. She couldn't, any more than Mair, imagine someone else in Ray's room.

"Zekia." The senior librarian continued. "The new Ray-Nor was seen in Kohoph yesterday?"

"Yes!" The eccentric scholar, her voice bursting with renewed excitement. "And yes, it is a third breach of pattern. One, a new Ray-Nor appears only a year after the previous one disappeared. Two," ticking a second finger, "this Ray-Nor doesn't look like a spider monkey, it looks like a gorilla. Three, it is not attached to just one librarian."

Tarn's eye shone with interest. She knew the history of Central Library, the plague of monsters that had wreaked havoc and death a year ago in Prahak. She also knew that the junior librarian named Ray had mysteriously disappeared despite a Ray-Nor's protection. Monsters in Prahak? Not the first occurrence. A Ray-Nor protecting a librarian from the non-humans affected by the winds in spring? It had happened a few times. But a librarian disappearing with a Ray-Nor had never been heard of before.

Working at Prahak Central Library was the dream of every librarian. Starting her career at Prahak Central Library was the best any aspiring librarian could ever hope for.

* * * *

Meanwhile, in his secret laboratory, Revek was throwing sampling bottles, flasks, Petri dishes, a random blow torch and some tubes with the strength of rage against the previously white wall.

Gorilla bibliothecarius was a complete failure. Gorilla bibliothecarius was not protecting just one librarian, but a second one in a nearby district. This failure of a monster was an altruist.

Revek grabbed handfuls of his sparse white hair and tried to pull them out.

III

Spring turned out to be the quietest one in years. The High Winds lacked their usual fierceness. Library customers, human and non-human, were on their best behaviour. Was the threat of a new Ray-Nor, one with the strength of a mountain gorilla, enough of an incentive for gentle attitude?

It was, except for one incident in the Southern part of Prahak, where the gorilla face was fortunately enough to rein in the temper of a Cthulhu creature – whose angry tentacles were already grabbing a librarian's neck.

In the midst of this quiet spell, Tarn was easing herself into the life of Central Library and Spider District. Soon, after hearing about the new junior librarian's degrees in feminist and lesbian literatures, Mair entrusted her with the non-official LGBTQ+ section. Lesbian, Gay, Bisexual, Transsexual, Queer, etc. These degrees, obtained before Library Science, explained why Tarn was older than most junior librarians. Her easy-going attitude and spontaneous smile made her quickly popular with most library users. Some even transformed their irregular presence into a weekly occurrence overnight. These included a quiet writer, whose published novels graced the library shelves, including the lesbian section. While she used several pseudonyms, her identity was no mystery to the librarians. Jarzi, who had always been polite while stern and absent-minded, started adding a shy smile to her usual nod when Tarn was on duty at the main desk of the public floor.

* * * *

"I am working on an essay," Zekia told Mair one morning. "With a focus on the Ray-Nor. Or Ray-Nors, I should say, because I doubt they'd have shapeshifting abilities."

"Have you found out anything new?" the senior librarian queried, her curiosity piqued.

"Not really," the eccentric scholar acknowledged with a sigh. "But if I correlate disappearances of librarians prior to apparitions of Ray-Nors, I can speculate. It is notable that in every occurrence, Ray-Nor activities stopped immediately at the end of a monster outbreak. The general pattern is: One, Ray-Nor, Two, monsters. In the 20th century and recently, a librarian was recorded missing roughly 13 months ahead of each of these events. The Ray-Nor and the monsters were always reported during the High Winds season."

"We haven't seen any monsters this year."

"And it puzzles me greatly."

"Have you spoken with the other librarians the Ray-Nor protected in other parts of Prahak?"

"Yes. They confirmed your description. Either it is the same Ray-Nor or each district has its own."

"Any idea where it would come from?"

"Its origins are open to speculations. And the monsters' origins, too."

* * * *

It was a quiet Sunday evening and there was laziness in the winter air. Tarn was walking to the home of an absentminded library user. With a Ray-Nor quick to the rescue, every librarian could feel unconcerned at the prospect of meeting a werewolf for the first time. Even though a Ray-Nor had never been seen in winter.

Boris Kershowski was known for his limited intelligence, so his current reading choice was no surprise. He lived in the poorest part of Spider District where broken windows were frequently replaced by a piece of cardboard or a plank of plywood. A working doorbell was more often than not a surprise.

When a dishevelled humanoid werewolf stepped outside after banging the door to the inside wall of the entrance, shaking the house foundations in the process, Tarn took an involuntarily step backwards. She saw the fury in the fierce eyes and automatically fell back into her librarian training.

"Good evening, sir. I am here representing Central Library of Spider District from the City of Prahak, regarding item number 1332, a book entitled 'The Werewolf of Fever Swamp'."

The werewolf growled. It was a sound galloping up his throat with promises of sharp fangs.

The gorilla Bibliothecarius dropped from the gabled roof on top of the werewolf. The creature writhed and hissed under the Ray-Nor, claws scratching the pavement, and howled a pitiful howl. He could barely breathe under his attacker's weight.

Mouth half open, eyes wide, the bewildered junior librarian stared at the Ray-Nor who attempted to smile, but its smile was more like a rictus.

The werewolf's growl mutated into quiet cries of frustration and his claws tightened into fists weakly hammering the cobbled ground.

The Ray-Nor slowly shifted its weight off Boris. Tarn saw a peaceful humanity in its eyes.

Soon, Tarn was heading back to Central Library with the book safely in her custody, and the Ray-Nor was nowhere to be seen.

IV

February showed bright colours in the main hall of Central Library. Oil paintings and framed inks by a local artist named Jo, who specialized in portraits, but was not adverse to landscapes and abstract.

The three librarians were amazed by the lifelike portrait of the current Ray-Nor and frequently after hours would just stand in front of the canvas. El was the most in awe as she had never found herself in a situation warranting a rescue.

* * * *

Mair was padding softly in the corridor leading to the kitchen. It was close to midnight and she didn't want to disturb her friends. Tomorrow was the longest work day of the week. She noticed a thread of light shining under Tarn's door, and then she heard Tarn's voice: "Yes, I have seen it. It looked like a silverback with a tail."

A silence. *She is probably talking over the phone, catching up with a friend*, Mair thought, walking on to the kitchen for a midnight snack. She didn't hear what Tarn said next.

"The scholar asked to interview me tomorrow. She's met with every librarian who has ever dealt with a Ray-Nor, but I don't think she knows much. I'll try to find out what she knows."

Tarn listened to a reply before speaking again. "No, no monsters yet. The scholar is puzzled about it. She's also puzzled about a Ray-Nor showing up in winter. The temperatures are milder than usual."

(…….)

"I'll call as soon as I know more."

Tarn switched her phone off and yawned. Her room was small, but she understood why Mair and El chose not to give her Ray's room. Even though the missing librarian was to never come back, she had worked at Central Library for seven years. Tarn would stay only as long as her assignment required. Then she would find an excuse to move on. She liked Mair and El and was enjoying passing as a librarian. She had a great respect for their commitment. Tarn's was to monsters. The good ones and the bad ones. Her secret organization – simply known as the Secret Society to people in the know – was about gathering knowledge and protecting monsters from the humans, and humans from the monsters. They had looked for a foothold in Prahak for as long as she had worked as an agent. Prahak was the golden assignment that every agent coveted.

She quickly logged in some notes in her multiple-password-protected smartphone and got ready for a night of deep slumber.

* * * *

Voice stumbling over unruly words at first. "Could I have a pencil, please?" Jarzi asked, smiling her shy smile and trying to keep eye contact with the junior librarian supervising the public room on that day.

"Sure," Tarn answered with a smile. She had once asked the writer what she did with every pencil she bought at every visit. Jarzi had blushed bright red and handed over a coin while looking away from the librarian. Mair and El had confirmed later: "Yes, she's got a crush on you."

Tarn had no idea how to handle the situation, beyond behaving as per usual. She liked the writer, but was not going to stay longer than her assignment needed.

How could a writer with such a bold style and outlandish ideas be so shy? Tarn had read most of Jarzi's books for years before coming to Prahak and admired the diversity and incisiveness of her body of work. She had even said so when officially introduced. Jarzi's embarrassment at the compliment had surprised her.

Half an hour later, the writer was back to the desk with a new query. "Would you have any books about Native-American artefacts? A book with photos, please."

"Of course," Tarn answered, beaming a smile at Jarzi while getting out from behind the desk.

Jarzi didn't like internet research and looked often puzzled when given directions to the appropriate bookshelves. So, Tarn would simply take her to the correct section, give her the reference number, and leave her there with another smile. She was a natural smiler. Jarzi was not, but would generally smile back.

Zekia arrived one hour later and Tarn ushered her to the rare manuscripts room under the unfocused gaze of the quiet writer. While unlocking a cabinet, Tarn arranged an appointment with the scholar and everyone went on with their day.

* * * *

At 4 pm, the bright young volunteer who had adopted the dog-crossed-wallaby canine joined Zekia in the rare manuscripts room.

"I adopted it as much as it adopted me. One day it was there by the entrance of Central Library. It seemed to be waiting for me. It followed me and actually looked disappointed when I left it outside. Eventually, after a few walks together, I invited it in. And it looked so happy! It had a huge smile. It behaves pretty much like a pet. Except that I have no idea what it does or where it goes when it is not with me."

"Like a pet, you say," Zekia said. "Did you give it a name?"

"Matane. It is a Japanese word. It means 'see you'. Because I always see it again at the end of the day."

"Do you study linguistics?"

"No." She shrugged. "I study Japanese philosophy. Actually, I was looking for the word 'smile', but Matane was a simpler word."

"And what does Matane look like?"

"If you come outside with me after this conversation, you'll see Matane." She smiled widely, apparently as smitten with Matane as Matane was with her. "It has the body of a dog and the head of a wallaby. I thought about it and it's more like a wallaby than a kangaroo. Kangaroos are a lot bigger than wallabies. Its fur is the same tan as a wallaby's. But its smile is more like a dog's, and it behaves like a dog. Oh, and when it's happy, it hops like a wallaby."

Zekia was taking notes, her handwriting as cryptic as a doctor's. She looked up and asked. "It is not male, not female either?"

"Nope."

None of the monsters and other mysterious creatures had a defined gender. If these creatures were not natural, someone was having fun in a genetic lab. Zekia had not been able to see El's feline on the roof. The skittish creature had run off without dinner at the scholar's appearance. Later, the junior librarian took several photos for Zekia to study.

After making sure that Tarn would lock up the rare manuscript she had been studying earlier, Zekia followed the enthusiastic young volunteer outside. There, Matane was, hopping on its canine legs and wagging its wallaby tail. The wide and happy smile of a pet dog across his wallaby face.

* * * *

"A silverback?"

"Yes, a silverback is an adult male gorilla. He protects his family and pretty much makes every decision for his group." Tarn explained.

"An adult male gorilla?" Zekia repeated with a frown. Tarn was the first librarian to describe the Ray-Nor in such words.

"No. I mean. Gorillas have no tail, by the way. It looks like a silverback gorilla, but with a tail. It still has no apparent gender. I think it is slightly smaller than a gorilla, but definitely taller and bulkier than a spider monkey."

"Okay. So, it dropped down from a roof."

"Yes! And between its weight and the law of gravity, the werewolf couldn't get up."

"Did it interact with you?"

"I think it smiled, but it looked more like a rictus."

"Did it say anything?"

"Aren't Ray-Nors mute?" Tarn froze for a second, wondering if she was supposed to know that, and went on. "It didn't say a word. From what I heard, Ray-Nors never speak."

Zekia looked at Tarn thoughtfully for a long moment before saying, "True, they've never spoken to anyone that we know of. They hiss, they growl, they snarl, but they don't speak. Muteness is a potential assumption. Do they have vocal chords? Could they hiss, growl, snarl, without vocal chords? I don't know."

"And......." Tarn ventured a question. "The other creatures? The monsters?"

"El's feline purrs. Kim's canine yaps. The flying monsters two years ago screeched. But no one ever said anything about the Ray-Nors. They don't even make....... monkey sounds. They hiss and snarl."

So, Tarn thought. *Zekia doesn't know more than we do.*

V

Spring arrived overnight with tuned spires singing louder than ever and High Winds all over the place. Library users were uncannily on time with returning items and librarians enjoyed a run of quiet evenings.

One morning, the quiet writer surprised Tarn by adding a few words to her nod and shy smile when she walked past the main desk. Half waffling, half sharpening words, she said, "Have you heard? Kolish is dead. He was attacked by a new monster last night."

The news spread all over Central Library and beyond, like wildfire through a tinder-dry forest at the height of a heat wave.

Actually, the religious zealot's body had not been found. Witnesses spying through windows from the safety of their homes had heard screams and watched as a creature on two legs, with the head of a crocodile and scales all over its body, dragged the terrified man away, leaving a trail of blood that led the police to a sewage grate.

"A bipedal saurian," said the eccentric scholar later while conferring with the three librarians, under the watchful eyes of a thoughtful Jarzi. Kolish's temper was not going to be missed, but the librarians and the scholar were humans and didn't wish harm to anyone.

46

"Homo Crocodylus," was Revek thinking in his secret laboratory, rubbing his hands with delight. He had mixed his own genes with those of a Nile crocodile.

* * * *

Tarn stepped out of the library through a back door, unaware of her watchers. It was a quiet evening. El was feeding the giant cat on the roof. Mair was dealing with administrative boredom. Tarn, being on kitchen duty, was on her way to one of the corner shops in search of exotic spices for dinner. It was twilight time. One watcher was walking along the edge of the roof, the other one was flying in circles.

She walked around the second corner and froze. A few steps away stood a bipedal saurian, eyes shining with malevolence and a smile broad with cruelty. Before Tarn could unfreeze, the monster jumped forward, but before it could reach her, the heavy weight of a gorilla Ray-Nor fell on its scales. And as Tarn was losing her balance, strong arms reached under her armpits and her feet lifted off the ground. She could feel herself being taken up and higher, but she couldn't see the creature saving her life. Was it a Ray-Nor, a *flying* Ray-Nor?

Tarn looked towards the ground and glimpsed the Ray-Nor and the saurian rolling over the dirty pavement. She was already flying above the rooftops. The air felt cool on her cheeks. A cat hissed. A murder of cawing crows startled her. And there she was, ungracefully dropped on the roof of the Central Library, a few feet away from El, who was staring at a retreating flying shape.

Tarn looked behind her and above her, but dusk was already hiding her saviour. "What was it?" She croaked.

El looked stunned.

"Did you see it? What did it look like?" Tarn asked, with a more articulated voice.

At last, El looked at her fellow librarian, eyes still amazed. "I'm not sure. I barely saw it. It looked human." She extended a hand to Tarn. "Are you okay? What happened?"

Tarn grabbed her fellow librarian's hand and pulled herself back to her feet. Her sore coccyx would survive.

"What happened?" El asked again, her grey eyes meeting the green ones.

Tarn's eyes unfocused and she shivered at the memory. "The bipedal saurian…" Her eyes refocused. "It was about to attack me. The Ray-Nor jumped down from the rooftops to stop it. The gorilla one. At the same time, someone, something, took me up into the air."

"Another Ray-Nor?"

"I don't know. I didn't see its face. I couldn't see it."

"It looked human. It was too quick. I mean…" She looked around. "The cat is gone. I mean, the cat hissed and ran away. The crows flew off. That's why I looked up. I saw you. And this… human-looking creature was already turning away and… yes. Flying away. I didn't really get to see its facial features. Just a flash of dark eyes. A silhouette against the sky. I don't know. Its wings… I don't know how to describe them. Not like a bird's. Not like a bat's either."

They looked at the sky. Dusk had turned into darkness.

Somewhere on the ground, in a nearby street, two unnatural creatures were fighting to the death.

VI

Tarn quietly made her way to the front of the gawking crowd watching the fantastic battle from a safe distance. Like most people, she had her smartphone out and started filming the two creatures. In the middle of the ah-oh-ing and wincing of the punters, she emailed the 15-second clip to her superiors. She was now wearing a light tan jacket hiding the improved gun strapped under her left arm. The fighting monsters punching and biting each other, rolling in the dust, were slowly moving towards a dark alley. Lampposts were now spreading glaring light around, but this light was not reaching the alley. When the inhuman fighters rolled into it, the noisy crowd hesitated. A male voice eventually said, "I'm calling the police!"

People slowly moved away and didn't notice Tarn silently stepping into the dark alley and letting the shadows swallow her. Loud grunting and ferocious growling bounced and echoed against the walls. Two metal skips banged against each other. Tarn had studied various maps of the area. She was aware of an abandoned storm drain at the bottom of the alley. It was supposed to be closed with a grill. Her eyes getting used to the almost darkness, she discerned the two silhouettes pushing each other into the tunnel.

She punched a quick text into her phone: *In pursuit. Underground. Tracker on. Send backup.*

* * * *

Jarzi's phone pinged loudly in her pocket. She read the new text: *Backup required now. Follow signal.* She clicked on the link. A map appeared on the small screen. A green dot following two red dots. She smiled. Time for a monster hunt. She knew the area and her eyes were well adjusted to the night. She spread her metaphysical wings – not bird's, not bat's, like shadows, but immaterial, delicate and diaphanous, flew off the roof into an arc, and dove into the dark alley, not even stopping the time of a heartbeat at the entrance of the storm drain. Her phone was beeping quietly. She was just a corner away. She landed and, with the modified gun the secret society had entrusted her with, her wings disintegrating into thin air, she walked around the corner. There she saw her favourite librarian pointing a gun at her and holding the Ray-Nor's gorilla head on her lap. The black fur of its chest looked sticky with blood flowing from several gaping wounds.

"You're the agent?" Jarzi murmured, dumbfounded.

Tarn was as dumbfounded and could only stare.

"I'm your backup." *Without hardly any field experience*, but she didn't say it out loud. She lowered her gun, mirrored by Tarn, and stepped closer. She kneeled down next to the duo.

The Ray-Nor moaned, its grey eyes filled with sadness and longing looking into Tarn's. It moaned weakly, a rumble deep in its throat.

"It is dying," Tarn whispered, stroking the fur on the gorilla's head. Jarzi looked at Tarn's face, then at the Ray-Nor's. It took a deep breath and stopped moving. The two wimin held their breath for a few seconds and exhaled at the same time. Tarn gently stroked the eyelids close and slowly, carefully laying the gorilla down on to the uneven ground, got on her booted feet. With a voice quiet, but strong with determination, she declared, "Let's find the bipedal saurian. And their cruel maker."

After a few steps, Tarn turned towards Jarzi and asked. "You're backup, okay. What's your skill?"

"I can fly."

* * * *

50

In the main room of his secret laboratory, bathed in bright light that wouldn't let any shadow hide, Revek was kneeling on the cement floor, cradling the mortally wounded bipedal saurian in his arms. The creature was looking at Revek's face with love and pain. Like all creatures created by the scientist, it had the emotional age of a toddler, but it was also special. The man had written its genetic patterns in such way that the bipedal saurian would always regard him as its mother and protect him if necessary.

One of the saurian's eyes was a wide mess of blood and mashed retina and cornea. A wound so deep that Revek knew the brain was damaged. The creature was covered with lacerations and blood – not just its. And Revek had grown attached to this one creature. Tears were slowly gathering into the tired eyes of the scientist.

Quiet and cautious footsteps made him lift his head as two wimin entered the high-ceilinged room.

"You!" He exclaimed. "Bloody librarian! My creature was meant to kill you! You and your kind! And next, stupid writer, you would have been next! You and all the other ignorant scribblers!"

He screamed, a scream that sounded more animal and more primal than human. The bipedal saurian tried to rise on its feet, but was too weak to lift even its head. The man pulled a gun out of his lab coat pocket.

Tarn and Jarzi fired at the same time. Jarzi's shot floored the mad scientist. Tarn's more powerful gun fired two shots that ravaged the chest of the monster.

Silence greeted the new deaths.

* * * *

Tarn and Jarzi walked all over Revek's secret laboratory and stared at many empty cells. In one vast room, they found many corpses in various states of decomposition. Monsters, winged and reptilian, were the most noticeable ones. In one corner close to the broad and high doorway, they found the skeletal remains of a human shielded by a humanoid with a tail.

Jarzi, who had researched on many subjects, including dinosaurs and animals, suggested that the humanoid was a Ray-Nor and the human a librarian. "The monsters must have tried to get to the librarian and the Ray-Nor protected her."

Her? Tarn didn't say anything. It was a possibility, of course. The librarian who had disappeared two years ago.

"The monsters must have fought among themselves, too."

They found the only creatures left alive in the secret laboratory in a different cell. It was an unaltered female crocodile and her babies. She snapped at them from behind the glass wall.

Another room turned out to be an office. There, they found digital documents, research notes on loose sheets of papers, hardback books and old manuscripts going back to the 18th century. All about genetics. A family affair?

Tarn called the Secret Society's headquarters, made a brief report and requested a clean-up crew.

* * * *

Spring felt like summer. Mair and El had been sad to see Tarn leave for another library, in a medium-size town in the south of the Prahak Shehrar Republic. Officially. Tarn had felt sad, too. She had loved working with them and she had loved being a librarian. She had also grown rather fond of the shy writer who could fly.

EPILOGUE

Two months later, Jarzi was doing the first book signing for her newest novel. Mair and El were over the moon that it was happening at Central Library. The event was well attended, by librarians and Jarzi's readers. They were surprised and delighted to see Tarn arrive in the middle of it.

"Couldn't miss it," Tarn smiled. "Jarzi is one of my favourite authors."

Officially, Jarzi was leaving for an international book-signing tour. But, in all truth, she was joining Tarn's secret society as a permanent agent.

IN THE SHADOW OF CENTRAL LIBRARY

In memory of Sirima (1964-1989)

Jo was walking away from the closing doors of Central Library, her mind swirling with impressionist images of wild animals and majestic oceans. Hands safely tucked into the pockets of her green jacket against the biting cold of early winter, a woolly hat hiding her short dark hair, she was walking on automatic pilot, from pool of light to pool of darkness. She was not afraid of darkness, she was just afraid of her boring life. Don't get her wrong. She enjoyed spending the afternoon sketching at the library and painting whatever her imagination would conjure and throw onto canvases.

She turned into a dark alley and found herself into one of the last huge vacant lots left in Spider District. It was puzzling that no estate developer had made a claim on it yet. Tendrils of fog stroked miserable grass and hugged rare skeletal trees.

At first it sounded like slow and quiet footsteps with an eerie quality. Then the sound mutated into horses' hooves, gently echoing in the evening fog, bringing Lipizzan horses from the Spanish School of Vienna to her artist mind.

Jo stopped and looked around, trying to locate the origin of the unusual sound. Her eyes scrutinized the light fog, inch by inch, until at last a form slowly took shape.

Really? She thought. *A pygmy mammoth?*

Prahak was no stranger to monsters, but this? In winter? She looked at the piercing red eyes directed at her. Red like fire, glowing with intensity.

"If I were you, I'd run," said a clear and confident voice behind her.

Jo almost jumped out of her skin. She turned around and saw a womon. She could see through her. A ghost? An astral projection? An hallucination? A 3D video communication? She looked familiar.

Jo refocused on the pygmy mammoth when she heard it noisily exhale air through its trunk and scratch the ground with a front hoof. It looked ready to charge.

"Really, run. This Baku means business. I'll deal with it."

Jo looked at her again, puzzled. The womon's hand made an impatient gesture as if to shoo her away. The Baku charged. Jo ran, her satchel banging against her jean-clad right buttock.

* * * *

Jo looked around the Prahak Great Hall. The explosion of bright colours fascinated her. She enjoyed vivid colours. Mostly on a canvas, at the tip of a paintbrush. This was the African Festival organised every two years. But why in winter? The choice of season felt like a contradiction to her. Was the Prahak council trying to discourage it? It was still popular. She caught up with her friend Tereki who had stopped at a stall to look at children's books. Tereki was as tall as Jo, about six feet, but with tight blonde curls framing a pale face. Tereki didn't like cold weather. Fortunately the Great Hall was well heated. While Jo had tucked her scarf away in her satchel, Tereki was still wearing hers around her neck, along with a ski jacket and a raincoat. Different people, different metabolisms.

After catching herself studying Tereki's long fingers gently stroking a picture in a book, Jo picked up a volume with a batik pattern framing a title and an author's name. But she was too distracted to read anything. Griot music was playing on the stage at the other end of the hall and mingled with people's conversations.

Tereki looked up and smiled at Jo. "Let's get some food."

"Yes!" Jo replied heartily, returning the smile. "Lead the way."

Before Jo could drown in the clear grey eyes, Tereki turned around and walked through the light crowd of the early evening. It was only Friday and the artist was glad of that. She trusted Tereki and felt safe with her. She valued her friendship. She rarely turned down Tereki's suggestions to attend events of any kind. How far would she follow her?

Jo's eyes were wandering the crowd, gazing at faces and –

"Jo?"

"Sorry." Jo refocused on Tereki while sidestepping a group of punters.

"Would you like to try some Nigerian food?"

"Sure." She noticed once again how relaxed Tereki was today. It was not always the case, but she couldn't figure out her friend's patterns.

Jo looked at the various dishes on offer, and being unfamiliar with Nigerian cuisine, was thinking about the item written out at the top of the board.

Was Tereki reading her mind? "Jollof rice is likely to be too hot for you."

"Ah." Jo's gaze swept over the dishes again. "Maybe beans and plantain porridge then."

"I think it is safe enough."

With their food on cardboard plates, they walked around in search of decent seating options and found a backless, faux leather sofa against a glass wall revealing a cobbled piazza and a gloomy sky over the baroque town hall. No snow.

They ate in silence, soaking in the background music – now some Senegalese drumming – and the general chatter. Jo's eyes wandered over the people walking past, from a stall of colourful ethnic clothes to another book stall, sometimes studying her friend's strong hands. Tereki was a carpenter.

"Any good?" Tereki queried after a few minutes between two mouthfuls of jollof.

"Satisfactory." Jo answered absentmindedly, lost in the sweet taste of plantain.

Tereki chuckled. She was used to Jo's understatements.

After another few minutes of companionable silence, Tereki exclaimed, "Did I tell you? I'm flying to Morocco next week!" It was news to Jo, and they both knew it. It was just Tereki's usual pattern of expression.

"Cool," said Jo. "Where about?"

"Marrakesh. I'll stay maybe three weeks."

Jo was now too busy chewing on a piece of plantain to comment. So, that was why her friend was so relaxed today. Three weeks were not that much, especially when they were seeing each other only once a month or so. But Jo couldn't help feeling a loss. Why? If they were just friends.

"Do you ever go on holidays?" Tereki asked.

"Yes." The artist's idea of a holiday was voluntary work in an animal sanctuary.

"Have you been anywhere this year?"

Jo hesitated. "No." And studied her last piece of plantain. She couldn't imagine painting fruits or flowers.

"How come?"

"Dunno. I think I missed the application window."

"For what?" Tereki looked at her with curiosity.

"Voluntary work at a donkey sanctuary. I'll go next spring."

"Working holiday?"

"Yes. I get bored otherwise."

Tereki smiled, amused.

Jo felt self-conscious. She knew exactly why she had been too late to apply.

* * * *

"Run!" shouted the ghost.

For once, Jo did as she was told to avoid being trampled by not just one, but two Bakus.

The ghost, who looked decidedly familiar, rushed towards the pygmy mammoths. Jo was too busy running to watch her rescuer phasing in and out of the Bakus, basically irritating them like a scourge of mosquitoes.

Jo slowed down when she reached the edge of the field. She spared a quick glance over her shoulder, but didn't see anything through the banks of fog. She trotted on until her home and felt grateful for living on the ground floor of a 60's building, despite the bars at the windows. Should she take up running as a regular activity? She unlocked the main door of the four-storey building and, falling back on habit, picked up a few envelopes littering the worn-out mosaic floor. A few bills for some of her neighbours, but nothing for her.

Three locks later, she was home and dropping her satchel on the uncluttered kitchen table.

When she had moved in, ten years ago, though she had not expected staying so long, she had taken the time to paint the walls. Fiery colours in the kitchen, flamboyant sunsets and sunrises in the front room, forests in the bedroom, and ocean islands in the bathroom.

Still breathing hard, she poured herself a glass of water from the filtered tap, drank it greedily and walked into the front room where she sat ungracefully on the old sofa covered with a green blanket.

She had barely recovered a normal heartbeat, when the ghost suddenly appeared between the coffee table and the flat TV screen.

Jo jumped. "What the..."

The ghost directed a stern gaze at her. Jo stared back. For two full minutes, they just stared at each other.

Eventually Jo broke the silence. "You look familiar."

The ghost turned her gaze up to the ceiling with irritation.

Now standing, Jo decided to switch the light on to chase the shadows away, while keeping her eyes on the strange visitor. "You look like Kural –"

"Irrelevant."

"I remember you busking by the Great Hall."

"Totally irrelevant."

"Okay." Jo shrugged. "What are you doing here? Are you a ghost?"

"Yes. It is the generic term. I accepted the assignment of protecting you from the Bakus."

"Backoos?"

"Baku. B, A, K, U. With an S for the plural."

"What are they? Why are they after me?"

Yes, she looked like Kural, the 25-year-old singer, murdered on the edge of stardom. Murdered by her jealous male partner. An uncompromising singer who didn't care about fame, but cared about doing her best. Kural's ghost? Jo studied the fine features with accentuated cheekbones, framed by long black hair. The small stature and strong presence. Born in Prahak, from a Shehrar mother and a Sri Lankan father.

Can ghosts sigh? Because it looked like this ghost just did. She seemed to recompose herself and when she spoke, here voice sounded even.

"Yes, I was Kural, but now it doesn't matter. Now, my name is Okami. I associated myself with the Ghost Guild of the Gambling Guardians."

"Gambling?"

Another sigh. "Please, do not interrupt. I have no answer for this question. The Guild has been around for a millennium. I wasn't there. The point is. We help – or attempt to – some humans to realise their potential. Generally, the humans hunted by Bakus."

Jo waited for more.

"Now would be the right time to ask me about the Bakus."

"You told me not to interrupt."

"Very literal of you."

"Yes, I can be so. So, tell me about the Bakus."

Kural/Okami nodded approvingly, almost smiling. She explained. "Bakus are from Japanese mythology. They are supernatural creatures who devour nightmares. According to legend, when the gods made every animal, they were left with parts and created the Bakus. Traditionally, Bakus can be summoned to deal with nightmares. If the nightmare isn't enough to satisfy their appetite, they are likely to feed on the summoner's secret hopes and positive dreams. You seem to be a choice morsel." The ghost moved about the room, giving the illusion of walking.

Jo scratched her neck with short nails and remembered she hadn't washed her hands. Her fingertips were dark and greasy with charcoal.

"Are you following?" Okami queried.

"Sort of."

"Good enough. Any questions?"

"Why are they after me? I haven't summoned them."

"Some Bakus have gone rogue. You are easy prey because of your low self-esteem. You are in denial."

"Denial of what?" Jo felt suddenly tense.

"One," said her rescuer, "you are in denial of your artistic talent."

Jo looked puzzled. And almost relieved. She wasn't sure why.

"I repeat: you are a talented artist."

"If I am really that talented, why are my closets full of unsold paintings?"

"You need to believe in yourself. Why don't you?"

* * * *

Jo was doodling in her sketching pad. Pygmy mammoths with thick hair on top of their head and tusks of warthogs. Or tusks of elephants. No, bigger. Mammoths, the ancestors of elephants, had huge tusks, and thick woolly coats. At the very least, the woolly mammoths had thick woolly coats. Or was it fur? It was definitely needed during the ice age. But a shorter trunk, from what she had seen. And rhinoceros eyes, according to the book she was consulting at the library, under the absent-minded gaze of the junior librarian on duty. Tarn, who was as tall as the artist, had never heard of the Baku, but she had known how and where to locate a dusty volume to satisfy Jo's curiosity.

The book also mentioned an ox tail and tiger paws and claws. Details she had no time to notice during her two encounters.

And she had assured her guardian ghost she had never said, "Baku-San, come eat my dream" in Japanese, in English or in Sherari. Not even once.

The conversation with Okami had turned into an intense and merciless psychotherapy session to discover the root of Jo's low self-esteem. The artist had homework: exhibit paintings somewhere ASAP. Okami believed in being proactive.

The book unearthed by Tarn from a locked cabinet Jo had never noticed before, was old, almost mouldy and slightly smelly. Once again, the artist was amazed by Prahak Central Library. In the book, she found ancient illustrations, woodblocks and parchments dating back to the middle-ages. Jo was fascinated.

Would a painting of a Baku sell? She suddenly wondered. And shook her head in dismissal.

She was still half-sketching and half-reading when El, the other junior librarian, a copper-haired womon smaller than her, sat at her table, smiling, and spoke softly. "Hello, Jo. Tarn mentioned you'd like to exhibit your paintings in our main hall."

Jo looked up and reconnected with reality. "Yes, I'd like that." She smiled. El's good mood was always contagious. Jo found it relaxing, as she had a tendency to feel life and everything else intensely, including –

"Well, we had a cancellation for February. Would it work for you?"

"Oh, yes!" Maybe Tereki would be around and come along and admire Jo's work and –

"I'll bring you the contract and the info right now."

That simple? Really?! Wow!

* * * *

It was January and winter had turned amazingly mild. Not a hint of snow had visited Prahak, but a Ray-Nor had rescued a librarian from a werewolf. Outside of spring. It was a first in local history. It was whispered within and without the walls of Central Library that Tarn, the junior librarian who had arrived less than a year ago, had been the lucky one.

Jo thought that maybe she could paint a Ray-Nor.

* * * *

Very aware that Okami had mentioned only one reason why the Bakus would be after her, Jo planned her art show with imaginary conversations with the ghost. The ghost would say this, the ghost would say that.

"Sure, I can help you," said Tereki in January when the artist innocently mentioned she'd need some help hanging the colourful canvases. They were in a Japanese shop where the tall blond womon frequently stopped by after a walk in Spider Central Park.

There could also be a private view arranged by the library as part of the exhibiting fee the librarians always apologised for. Budget cuts had been merciless the previous year.

Jo hadn't seen one Baku since starting the planning of her first solo show. What could another reason be? She'd rather not speculate about it.

No Bakus also meant no Okami. But Jo's imaginary conversations were enough.

* * * *

Jo had emptied her closets. Landscapes, animals, abstract. Oil paintings and framed inks. Almost a complete…. retrospective. The only portraits she had hung on the walls of the main hall at Central Library with Tereki's able help were of musicians and writers Jo didn't know personally. She had painted portraits of almost all of her friends – including Tereki – and gifted the final results to the subjects. Her two newest pieces were a herd of Bakus with a blue feel, and a soulful portrait of Kural fiery with life. She was surprised when Tereki recognised the murdered singer, whom most people had forgotten after 30 years. Tereki had studied the likeness for a long silence before murmuring, "I remember her. Such a tragedy. She was so gifted." She smiled the memory away. "You are so good at painting portraits."

"I try." Jo shrugged, looked away and blushed. She always enjoyed a compliment from Tereki. Her friend didn't notice. Jo made sure of that. She didn't want her to know how much she valued her opinion.

"Is that it?" Tereki asked. "Are they all up?" She looked around at the discarded bubble wrap crowding the polished parquet.

"Yes, that's it." Jo answered, refocusing on reality and admiring her colourful work.

They gathered the bubble wrap and left the building.

"Until the evening," said Tereki while starting her car.

And that evening, Jo was surprised to see how many people came to Central Library to eat peanuts and tartlets, drink wine and orange juice, and look at her paintings. Some were friends of Jo's, other library regulars, and even quite a few she had never seen. She knew the librarians had done a good job advertising the private view.

Tereki appeared next to Jo with a smile, but didn't stay long. She had forgotten a previous engagement and apologized for that. She gave Jo a warm hug and next Jo got distracted by a womon whom she recognized as a local writer. Jarzi was the name and the artist had read some of her books. She didn't see Tereki exchanged a few words with one of the junior librarians. Later, at the end of the evening, she saw a few paintings sported a 'sold' sticker on their price tag. It included Kural's portrait.

It was dark when Jo stepped outside. She was feeling good. And dreamy. Her feet knew their way home. She only realised she was walking across the vacant lot when she heard Okami's firm voice. "Run."

"What?" Her feet stopped moving. She looked around. Three Bakus were getting ready to charge. "What?" She repeated with surprise.

"Run!"

* * * *

Drinking a mug of green tea in her kitchen, Jo stared at the ghost almost resentfully while saying, "I did what you said. The private view tonight was, I'd say, a success. And well, I am feeling more confident about my art work. So, why are the Bakus still after me?"

Okami had a stern look about her. After a long minute, she broke the silence. "You tell me."

Oh oh, Jo thought. *Please, no.*

"I'm waiting." Okami looked like she was tapping a foot impatiently.

"Dunno," Jo looked away with an uncomfortable feeling.

"Are you going to deal with it or give yourself to the Bakus as a snack?" The ghost was now standing almost nose to nose with Jo. The living woman couldn't feel the immaterial ghost, but she sure felt crowded.

The artist reflexively pushed herself to the back of her chair with a thud.

"Fine," said Okami. "I shall spell it out for you. T, E, R, E, K, I."

Jo felt herself blush beyond the roots of her short hair.

"What are you going to do about it?"

Jo mumbled something unintelligible, her throat tight with a knot.

"I can't hear you."

Jo sighed. And whispered, "Dunno."

"Ha. Humans."

"How do you know anyway? And weren't you human once?"

"I am a member of the Ghost Guild of the Gambling Guardians. We know everything. And I was human, yes, several times."

"Several times?!"

"Nice diversion. Now, back to your feelings for Tereki."

"You know she is out of my league."

"Tsk, tsk."

Jo's eyes focused on the mug of tea trembling in her hands.

"Out of your league? Since when?" The ghost was almost shouting.

"Since forever."

"Really?"

"I'm not worth it. She deserves better."

"But she's friends with you."

"I'm feeling very lucky about it."

"Luck has nothing to do with it. She chose to be friends with you as much as you did."

"I don't know why she'd choose to be friends with me, but I sure won't complain about it."

"What do you like about her?"

Jo's face involuntarily relaxed. "There is something about her energy, her aura. I can't explain it. I couldn't take my eyes away from her the first time I saw her."

"But you didn't talk to her. Why?"

"I'm shy. Besides, who'd want to talk to me."

"Jo. Point number one: you have friends and they do better than talking to you, they talk *with* you. Point number two: Tereki talked to you."

Jo remembered how speechless she had felt when the amazing woman walked up to her and introduced herself. They were in a club, the music was loud and Jo could barely hear the beautiful stranger's voice, but they were both there for a friend's birthday. The same friend. Their conversation turned out limited and banal. Jo's mind was blank. She blamed the loud music, but knew she was stunned by Tereki's smile.

"Jo?" Okami's voice brought Jo's mind back to present time. "What are you going to do about it?"

"About what?"

"Come on, Jo! She didn't talk to you to be polite. She talked to you because she wanted to. You're shy, but so is she. The main difference between you and Tereki is that her self-esteem is healthier than yours."

"What do you want me to do?"

"Jo, you are simply infuriating."

Jo looked away.

The ghost sighed. "Are you really happy with this…. Status quo of yours?"

"Yeah. Besides, if she wanted…. Well…. If…. I guess being friends is fine with her, so I'm happy with it."

"You're lying, Jo."

"Look. If she wanted…. Something else, she'd have said so ages ago."

Okami grumbled, "You're gonna have to do better than that to convince me." If the ghost had physical feet, she'd be thudding a heavy metal beat by now.

Jo looked down at the kitchen floor and sighed. "I'm a romantic. This world is not for romantics. Maybe it'd be better for everyone if I was dead."

The dead singer threw her arms out in disgust. "No wonder the Bakus want you for elevenses!" Okami had no lungs, but she

68

took a deep breath nonetheless. And two more to feel calm enough to speak with a relatively neutral tone. "And this is why I'm here. To help you become a remarkable and confident womon that everyone will love."

Jo's right eyebrow lifted up in an expression of doubt.

"Wait and see. I am barely getting started."

* * * *

"Smile," the ghost had said. "When you read a book. When you study a painting. When you talk with a friend, an acquaintance, or even a stranger. When you are awake at night. When you watch the news on TV. When you miss the bus. When you drink coffee, even if it tastes like cat piss. Smile all the time. Your facial muscles will be grateful! Go to a park and hug a tree, with your entire being. Even if people stare at you like you're a freak. Be proud to be a freak!"

So, Jo smiled at her reflection in the mirror every morning while brushing her teeth. She smiled at the grumpy religious zealot, who stopped in his tracks, puzzled, on the steps of Central Library. She smiled to Mair when the senior librarian frowned while saying, "Sorry, this book is currently out." She smiled when her friend Karla showed her photos from the private view. She smiled, albeit with a hint of sadness, when she heard about the religious zealot's demise at the teeth of a bipedal saurian. She smiled when she received her overestimated water bill. She smiled while listening to the High Winds' song heralding the arrival of spring.

* * * *

The artist felt elated and optimistic. She was looking forward to the Saturday gig where a local lesbian band was going to launch their brand new album. A few of her friends would be there, including Karla with her camera, and, of course, Tereki.

Canned music was playing when Jo ordered a tequila mixed with pineapple juice and lemonade at the bar, smiling at the gay bartender barely out of his teens.

"Jo! How are you doing?" Tereki was smiling and Jo smiled back warmly, hugging her friend. There was something carefree about the tall womon with short blond hair, a sparkle in her grey eyes the artist was not used to. And Tereki said, "This is my friend Yera." She was holding hands with a womon with long red hair and sharp cheekbones.

"Nice meeting you," Jo said, shaking the womon's free hand, still smiling with her entire being, but with something frozen inside herself.

A drum roll resonated through the speakers, bringing the canned music to a halt and ending the handshake. Everyone looked to the stage where a drag queen showing off a blonde wig reminding Jo of Dusty Springfield, and a sequined evening dress dazzling like the finest Motown vocalists' outfits, picked a microphone and greeted the crowd of eager punters with extravagant words.

* * * *

Jo was still smiling when she got home, where the ghost was waiting for her expectantly. Without a word, but with dreamy eyes, the artist sat in her old armchair.

The ghost impatiently broke the settling silence. "Have you told Tereki? How did she react?"

"No."

Okami frowned. "What do you mean, no?"

"I haven't told her."

70

"What? Why?"

Jo looked directly into the dark eyes wide with surprise and worry. "She's got a girlfriend."

"What are you going to do about it?"

"Nothing."

Slowly. "What about the Bakus?"

Still smiling, Jo answered, her voice hard with confidence. "Let them come. I'll make blankets out of their hides."

THE LAST ONE LEFT TRAVELLING
(edited by Jennifer L. Miller and previously published in the Ladies and Gentlemen of Horror 2017)

CHILDREN OF THE SAND
(edited by SW Fairbrother and previously published in the anthology Another Place in 2018)

THE LAST ONE LEFT TRAVELLING

For Aleppo, may you see peace and prosperity again

Intro

"Kajdar!"

The voice sounded familiar. There was a smile in it. I stood there for a moment, disoriented and bleeding profusiously, amazed by my surroundings: a room in exceptionally good shape. Maybe everything was too out of focus for me not to fantasize about a bed with a colourful quilt and tidy, but full bookshelves. I turned around, fighting a wave of nausea. The woman's smile froze when she saw my ravaged chest. She looked familiar, but my brain was a headache and my vision was blurry. I could only guess a reddish blonde pony tail. She recovered and helped me down to the floor after grabbing a red cushion to separate my head from the green carpet. She looked around and walked away. She came back quickly with a pale green towel to soak the blood from my chest.

Did I blink? Standing by the door, she was speaking into an interphone, "Fran! Kajdar is here! Bring your med kit!" Her knees back to the floor by my side, she whispered, "Fran is on her way. You'll be alright. This is Reality 4." I hadn't seen Reva with a pony tail for a long time. Strands of hair neatly tucked within a black velvet tie. Or was it a simple rubber band? Her grey eyes were focused on mine. They seemed to be swirling. Or maybe I was spinning.

75

I fell into darkness.

Ch 1

Her misty grey eyes were staring up at me. "I cannot see you." She tried to lift her hands. Her fingers moved, weakly, almost searching the air. "I cannot feel you." Her voice sounded like a torn throat. "But I know you are here."

Kneeling in the rubbles of the house recently eviscerated and charred by another volley of mortars and ignoring the sharp fragments digging into my knees, I was holding her bleeding head and her broken upper body against my chest. The skin exposed by the torn shirt was rapidly going cold against my warmth.

She shivered. "You have to keep going." Her voice was barely a whisper now.

I caught her last breath with a sad kiss. I turned my face up to the sky crowded with clouds and cried a loud roar. Pain was blinding my eyes. I was the last one left to make the Keltoks pay. In Reality 1. And I would Travel. In the footsteps of Reva. In the footsteps of Kayla. I was the last one left Travelling…

Ch 2

I watched Kayla walking past 1950's cars damaged and rusty, missing their wheels, their windshields broken. She was navigating with a sure footing among the rubbles, in the sad remnants of a neighborough we had known well. I flittingly wondered how many people had exhaled their last breath, trapped under layers of broken bricks and concrete. A bird flapping its wings made her look up. I could see the tension in her shoulders. I wondered what her name was in this Reality and what this Reality was. The Keltoks had been here and were still using our city as a feeding ground; otherwise she wouldn't need to carry weapons. I looked at the irate scar crossing down her damaged right eye under her short dark curls. This was the wound that had killed my Kayla. She had been the first one to die. It had broken my heart and Reva's. Now my Reva was dead and my heart was so broken I couldn't count the pieces. I was alone and I had no choice but to travel.

I stepped out from my hiding spot behind the last vestige of the brick wall of a gutted house. Her riffle immediately pointed at me, ready to fire.

Her left eye stared, deep brown unbelieving. She slowly lowered her weapon. "Kajdar. I watched you die......."

"And I watched you die. Which Reality is it?"

She frowned, standing next to a leafless tree, whose broken branches hung miserably. "How many realities do you expect?"

"I don't know. Several Realities, parallel to each other. I am from what I call Reality 1."

"So, you are not my Kajdar......."

"And you are not my Kayla."

"My name is Chatran."

"Okay. Where is.......?" I hesitated. What was Reva's name here? Was she still alive? "In my Reality, we are three. I am the last one."

Chatran's eyes darkened and looked away. "Devar died last week."

A spectral laughter echoed in the ruins surrounding us.

"The keltoks!" She whispered, suddenly alert, her left eye scanning our surroundings.

A lightning exploded in front of me. I suddenly felt torn apart. It was just a blast of motion sickness while Travelling from one Reality to another.

I shakily stood up on the rubble fighting the urge to vomit. I gave up some acid bile while hanging on to what was left of a wall to keep my balance. Wiping my mouth with the back of my left hand, I looked around at the ruins of the house I was standing in. The sky was a huge mass of grey clouds over its missing roof. Another world destroyed by the Keltoks. Keltoks didn't get their hands dirty. They psychically infected people and drove them against each other, drove them to terrorist attacks and suicide bombings, wars in the name of a peaceful god and mass killing in schools and airports.

This didn't feel like my Reality. I looked to the street across the missing external wall. On my left a few feet away, a Victorian building in apparent good shape, aside from the broken stained glass of its front door, one of the last panes of glass left wobbling in the city. On my right, it was rubbles upon rubbles with not a wall standing. As far as I could see, there was no human being anywhere. I stepped out of what might have been a small house. I seemed to always land in a destroyed building. But then, there wasn't any other kind of structures left. I remembered the three of us huddled together at night. Kayla, and later Reva, whispering about their Travels, their nonsensical quality and their timelines getting warped. They never knew where they would land, nor when. Sometimes, they would stay five minutes, sometimes a week, and occasionally longer. But they would always come back to our Reality at some point. So far, I hadn't. They had never met their alternative selves. When Kayla had died, Reva had inherited this 'Travelling' gift. And now I was the unlucky heir.

Stepping onto the uneven and treacherous broken pavement of the street, and walking towards modern buildings that hadn't turned into rubbles yet, I kept listening to the silence. Had the Keltoks fed on the last ounce of energy of the last human being here? If they had, what was I doing here?

"Kajdar?" A familiar voice whispered with surprise behind me.

I slowly turned around and stared into Reva's grey eyes. Sure, she was not my Reva, but she was....... I briefly wondered why, so far, my alternative selves had the same name in the Realities I had visited, but not my friends. I wondered, could she fly? I had not heard any foot steps.

"Kajdar? Is that really you?" There was love in her whisper.

I smiled gently. "Yes, and no."

She frowned, puzzled.

"I am Kajdar, but from a different Reality."

"From a different reality," she repeated. She looked away, breaking our staring contest.

I noticed a scar, red and angry, like a dried river flowing along her hairline down the left side of her face. "Are you Reva? Or Devar? What is your name?"

"Vreda."

We heard voices. Male voices. We looked around. They were not in sight yet. Probably still on the other side of the nearest corner.

Vreda didn't hesitate, she grabbed my hand. "Come with me!" Like my Reva, her power was flying. We were barely touching the ground, barely scraping the rubble, and weightlessly scaling the air up.

The men came round the corner too soon. "There!" They armed their riffles.

I turned around on well honed reflexes and extended one arm. Fire sprouted from my hand and flew like a rocket, taking two of their weapons. And again. They cried out in disbelief and anger. One man screamed with pain, his right arm on fire. Ah! Memories of Kayla twisting weapons and redirecting my fire with the power of her thoughts flooded my mind.

Vreda's power kept us levitating away from them, now five feet over the uneven surface. Vreda dropped us to the ground behind a garden wooden fence still standing.

The screams, voices and foot steps of the men disappeared in the distance.

I looked into Vreda's haunted grey eyes. "Where is……. Kayla? Chatran?"

Guessing, she answered, "Shelar died a few weeks ago."

We had no time for tears, but sadness was a heavy presence. I wanted to ask about my alternative self, her Kajdar.

"You died in my arms. Last week."

She was the last of her Triad, too. "Can you Travel to other Realities? Other dimensions?"

"No. How do you do that?"

Not knowing how long I would stay in her Reality –Reality 3– I pressed on. "The Keltoks?"

"What about these monsters?"

"They've been in every Reality I visited. And they're winning……. I'd like to find a Reality where I can make them pay."

"So, you're not staying." I heard the disappointment in her voice as she looked down at the scuffed tips of her dusty boots. I wanted to curl up with her in the night.

"I have no control about how long I'm staying nor which Reality I'll visit next." I was only a visitor. With no anchor, no beacon to call me home. When Reva died, my home, my Triad, died with her.

(Interlude) Wars are battles between two opposite factions, frequently started by the most extremist regardless of their faith. Our city had been flourishing, a cultural beacon in our country, its architecture reflecting a diversity of influences. Maybe I should have been proud of its open-mindedness, the differences cohabitating almost harmoniously, but it is too late to think about it. Hatred is a virus. It starts small, then expands. It started with words, graduated to fists and moved on to weapons. Neighboroughs turned against neighboroughs, neighbours against neighbours, siblings against siblings. Kayla, Reva and I witnessed skirmishes, tried to mediate and quickly felt powerless. We started losing legal rights, and foreign bombs fell on churches, mosques and other temples, governmental buildings, schools and libraries. The wounded had barely been taken to hospitals and the dead buried, that a fresh bleeding intake was taking its turn. Kayla, Reva and I helped, driving ambulances, loading gurneys, wrapping wounded with bandages. We also carried illegal guns concealed in our pockets.

Then the hospitals fell. Doctors, nurses, medics and volunteers became too angry to help, their compassion eaten away by hatred. The last wifi tower crashed to the ground, crushing a dozen people in the process. Why were we not affected? Standing in the middle of our declining city, we watched the population dwindle, we watched rioters and gangs, destroying and fighting. A blow to the head sent Kayla Travelling for the first time.

Ch 4

Mortars and grenades flying and exploding around me told me I had landed in the middle of a battleground. Two factions, their minds poisoned by the Keltoks, were fighting for ruins and rubbles, remnants of imperfect worlds.

I wondered where to run for cover. The next explosion was so close that it pushed me into a brick wall that crumbled into dust and debris. My chest was on fire, and the next jump ripped me apart. *Death,* I thought fugitively, *would be so welcome.*

Ch 5

That's how I landed in Dany and Fran's Reality. For me, it was my first visit to Reality 4, my first encounter with them; for them, it was their third. Time can be so complex and so confusing.......

The next time I opened my eyes, they eventually focused on cheekbones and dark curls. Kayla? No, the curls were too long. In my Reality, short hair, often shorn close to the skull, was the practical fashion for most fighters. It was war. Here........ Maybe the Keltoks hadn't been here yet.

The womon smiled. "Hey, I'm Fran."

I just stared at the warmth in her eyes. I wondered if Fran and the other womon had the same powers as my Kayla and my Reva. I wondered where their Kajdar was. I wanted to drown in her soft brown eyes.

"Where am I?" I eventually mumbled. My throat felt as parched as the Sahara.

"You are in Reality 4, and you're going to be fine. We know you because it is our third encounter with you."

"No, I mean." Speaking was painful, thinking was a torture, but I had to know. "I mean, my equivalent. The other Kajdar. Your Kajdar."

Her smile faded. "We have no idea."

No Triad here……. I closed my eyes and my consciousness shifted.

Several times, while lying on my sick bed, I felt the painful pull of the Jump, but I didn't Jump, I stayed. I have no idea why. Maybe Travelling required my physical energy and I was too weak. Every time I'd wake up, Fran, or the pony-tailed Reva, was watching over me. I would dwell in their eyes wishing to forever lose myself in their compassion, wanting to find out more about their identities and their Reality. I was too weak to organize ideas into words and sentences. So I would just revel in the touch of fingertips on my forehead or the feel of a hand gently closing around mine.

(Interlude) Desperation triggered my power. I was lying on the ground by a wall, rubbles poking at my back, my knife too far from my fingertips. A man with a crazy rictus decorating his face was walking towards me, my riffle confidently held by his hands. Desperation turned into determination. I was down, but I was not done. My attacker fell in the crossfire of Kayla's volley of bullets and the fire suddenly rocketing out of my fingers. The human torch stumbled and fell next to me. Reva quickly dragged me a few metres away. We were stunned. Kayla travelled between dimensions and I could project fire… Kayla and I looked at Reva, the three of us wondering what her power would be.

An explosion behind a tall, empty and damaged-beyond-repair building broke through our thoughts. Picking up my weapons, we ran for cover in what was left of our local library.

Ch 6

Feeling nauseated and dizzy, I leant against a convenient brick wall with fragments of plaster and the remnants of an unidentifiable poster. I could hear the repetitive fire of an AK47 nearby, and the replying shots of an automatic gun. The sound of a freshly hit pipe spouting water. Vreda appeared in my field of vision. I don't know what she saw when her eyes found me, but I saw the pain distorting her face, the blood gushing through her fingers clutching her right shoulder. The gun slipped out of her right hand.

What did I look like with bandages wrapped tight all around my torso?

Vreda slid to the ground, still a few metres away. I heard a spectral laughter. She didn't react.

Too weak to do more than hug the wall to keep upright, I was powerless to save her from the Keltok greedily hovering around her. I could see through its translucent, monstrous shape. It was humanoid with sharp teeth, always ready to devour. I saw a flash of red fire in the orbits of its hooded eyes. Skeletal hands like claws clutching Vreda's shoulders, it closed its jaws around her neck and started to feed, aware of my presence and oblivious. I watched the life fade out of her eyes, her grey irises turning white around the infinite pools of her pupils. I wanted to scream, but couldn't. My next Jump tore me away with pain exploding in my lungs.

Ch 7

I opened my eyes to see Fran watching me. She smiled. "Good, you're awake."

84

I knew she wasn't my Kayla or Chatran because, while she had the same cheekbones, her dark curls were longer, her jaw and shoulders were not as square, and her skin looked softer. She didn't know war.

Her eyes moved their attention away from me and she called, "Dany!"

And Dany wasn't my Reva, nor Vreda. Reva had cut off her pony tail a long time ago and she had bitter lines at the corners of her mouth.

They gently helped me to sit up. I was in Dany's room again. There was such positive energy there that I would have smiled and relaxed, if not for my blown-up chest. Well, that's how it felt.

"Okay," Fran said. "We're going to help you to a bed. Before I give you a sedative, I'll change the bandages and we'll tell you where you're at. And when." I felt something wet and warm slowly seeping through my bandages. She added, "you're here for a few weeks."

A few weeks? How could she know?

They helped me up, each sliding under one of my arms, and walked me out of Dany's room and through a corridor lined with wooden panels. We then stepped into the infirmary. They helped me sit down on a cot, and before I could lie down, Fran started to carefully unwrap my blood-soaked bandages.

Dany was talking. "This is Reality 4. This is your second visit here. However, and this is no spoiler, our near future is your past, and your near future is our past." I must have looked puzzled, because she smiled, while pain burst in my chest and Fran swiftly applied a thick piece of gauze to my bleeding wound and whistled a single, long note at the sight of the fresh scarring zigzagging all across my chest. So fresh, that it had re-opened in some parts.

Dany went on. "The next time we see you, it'll be your first time, but we'll be ready for you."

"But before that, in three weeks' time, you'll jump to another dimension. When you'll come back to our Reality, then it'll be the first time we'll see you. Do I make sense?"

I looked at the syringe in Fran's hand and closed my eyes, trusting in their care.

(Interlude) Reva discovered her flight power when a man pushed her off a flat roof. Kayla's mind threw an unhinged door at a group of men when she ran out of munitions, her back against a wall. We learnt to control our powers and combine them together. We were a team. We were a Triad.

We watched our families and friends fall in a spray of bullets or fall with a knife lodged in their backs. No one was safe, no one felt safe. Between the neighbours turning on everyone and the war waged upon us by an extremist state, one couldn't trust a stranger any more. And the Keltoks...

The first one we ever saw was feeding on Kayla's mother. We were too late. She had walked too close from an exploding bomb. She was covered with blood, still breathing, but unconscious. A Keltok was sucking on her neck with great concentration. Kayla threw a piece of rubble at its transparent shape. The half-brick flew through. We ran, but we were too late and we knew it. The creature took flight with a burst of spectral laughter echoing in our destroyed neighborough. My fire burnt through its ghostly shape. Reva couldn't catch it: it was immaterial. Kayla was holding her mother's corpse, softly crying.

We learnt to recognize the signs. Soon, we were the last people left unscathed. I am not sure why. The Keltoks manipulated people so they could feed on the dying. They didn't care about dogs

86

or cats. Animals learned to be weary of infected humans, and all humans, to be safe.

We called them the Keltoks because of this strange sound we'd hear sometimes when one was nearby, or when an infected gang was getting close. Our homes were no longer safe and most shops had already been looted several times and left empty and desolated. We were rarely hiding in the same place every night. We had become fighters. But why stay? We tried to leave, to run away from the only city we had ever known, but it was under siege. We saw many people disappear in the fires of explosions on the outskirts of a city that still so recently had been a beacon of culture and education.

Ch 8

I arrived in Reality 2 just on time to knock out a possessed human by falling on top of him and grinding his face into sharp debris. The gun trained on Chatran flew free out of his hand and ricocheted against a wall, firing a bullet towards the sky. My friend had lost her footing on the rubbles and landed in an empty doorway, her hands suddenly empty from her weapons.

I took a deep breath and exhaled slowly, recovering from the wrenching pain dealt by the inter-dimensional travel. Chatran looked at me, a smile shaping on her tense features. My left hand reached to the wall for support. It was wobbly. I righted myself quickly.

Three weeks in Fran's care had done wonder to my chest wounds. My fresh scars had tensed, but held.

Chatran recovered her weapons and stood up. The scar across her right eye looked angry. I picked up the unconscious man's gun. His face was crushed. His breathing was ragged. I wanted to hug Chatran tight, but there was no time for that. Evening was approaching. We didn't wish to cross path with his friends or with a Keltok. We didn't care if this man was now food for a Keltok. These men had no scruples when it came to wimin and children.

She motioned for me to follow her through the ruins. The adjacent building, while lacking doors and windows, still went a few floors up. Regardless of the Reality, she was one of my Triad, I trusted her and she trusted me. We walked into the building, careful to step over sharp rubbles and potential traps. The ghastly laughter of a Keltok feeding echoed in the descending light. We swiftly stepped into the shadows.

I quietly whispered, "The Keltoks haven't touched every Reality yet." I felt her good eye focus on me. "While I can only Travel to Realities where my equivalent is dead, I went to one where your equivalent and Devran's live in a house in good shape. Fran, your equivalent, is a doctor. A good one."

An explosion in a building a few blocks away shook the wall next to us. We looked at the wide and empty door frame, listening. She grabbed my hand and pulled me into the opposite direction, through a narrow door frame. We checked our weapons and waited, standing next to each other, our bodies touching. A feeling of familiarity so strong that I would have held her tight, if not for the danger lurking nearby.

_Ch 9_

Fran stared at me, shocked at my sudden appearance, her eyes reflecting her ignorance regarding my identity. Once again the inter-dimensional Travel had torn me away from a Reality and jolted me into another. My head banged against a wall. I winced, feeling sick.

"Hey," I managed to croak. "Good to see you again." I rubbed the nascent bump on the back of my head and took a deep, slow breath to settle my stomach, contemplating my bearings. This time I was not in Dany's room. It looked like an office, or a study. I saw bookshelves hiding a wall. Maybe a library.

"What?"

Ah, how relaxed she looked, even on the alert, contrary to Kayla and Chatran. But as beautiful. And I loved her as much. It flashed through my mind, that the only hope of humanity against the Keltoks was a Triad like I used to be with Kayla and Reva. I had to find out where my equivalent was. I had to convince Fran and Dany.

"Where is Dany?"

"Who the hell are you?"

I shook the ringing in my ears. "I am Kajdar."

"I don't know you."

I almost felt like laughing. So much work to do. I had the advantage to know her future, even if not all the details. I also knew how to convince her; her future self had told me.

I heard a distant sound, pulsating and shrilling. When she had stepped towards her desk and grabbed its edge, she had pressed a hidden switch and called security. What an interesting school she was working in.

"Fran, I need you and Dany like a fish needs water. And you both need me."

A door slammed open behind me and I turned around. Dany, her face flushed from running, was now here, too. I extended my arms away from my body to show them how harmless I was. I realized that my left hand was still holding the gun I'd been shooting with in Reality 2. I slowly deposited it on the polished wooden floor. "Hey, Dany."

Dany stared at me, tension running along the line of her jaw. I couldn't help but smile.

"I've met the two of you before, but it is the first time you meet me. I know it sounds weird, but–"

Someone else stepped into the room. My eyes found two wimin in dark simple outfits with the word 'Security' embroidered on their shoulders. They were muscled, they were trained fighters. Dany was not, but she couldn't help running to Fran's rescue in case of danger. And so would Fran for Dany. And so would I for Kayla, Reva and their equivalents in any Reality. This was how Kayla and Reva had died. It was a dangerous quality that made me love them even more.

Ch 10

Reality 2 again. Can I only travel to Realities where at least one of them is alive? A Reality where I will not bump into any of my other selves? It had been the same for Kayla and Reva.

Chatran was pleased to see me, and so was I. We would have hugged, but every ruined building was a potential minefield, especially during the daytime. The feelings are the same from one Reality to the next. It is the power of the Triad. The connection with Chatran was there; I needed to strengthen it with Dany and Fran. But right now, I was fighting with Chatran, and it felt good. It felt familiar and natural. I could have lost myself in it with gratitude. If it was not for the gang of men infected by the Keltoks. We had to kill them to survive. Once infected, people were doomed. It was a catch 22: dying, they became sustenance for the

Keltoks. The never-ending Keltoks. Ghostly scavengers from another world.

We were slowly walking between what was left of small structures, trying not to kick rubbles or make a sound, our eyes everywhere and on everything. Our route was a wide circle to avoid narrow streets and their protruding steel and unstable concrete, and to escape the gang. We could hear them in the distance. Nightfall was close. A temporary shelter was close.

A heavy weight fell on top of me, and gravity dropped us noisily to the uneven ground. Chatran turned around, and in one jump rushed my attacker, her momentum lifting him off of me. They rolled away and I saw a nasty grin shape on the man's dirty face. His knife was skewering Chatran's abdomen.

I screamed her name, running to them, and painfully exploded.

I was still screaming her name when I landed in Reality 4.

Ch 11

I emerged from the fog of pain cradled in Fran's arms. It felt odd to have my eyes recovering focus on the live version of someone whose death I had just witnessed. While Fran had no scar crossing her right eye and her dark curls were almost touching her shoulders, to me, she was Chatran, she was Kayla. I had watched them die. I had felt the pain of their death. It is like having your heart ripped out of your chest while it is still beating.

Dany was kneeling with us, completing the group hug. Their hearts beating with mine, comforting it.

My mind felt blank and confused. My Triad was dead. My Triad was alive. But Fran, Dany and I were not a Triad yet. Fran and Dany were together. Their relationship, their bond, was deep and strong, but it was incomplete, and they knew it now, they had always suspected so. My body, my mind, my entire being, was calling to them, tugging at their cores, pulling their heart strings. And they knew it.

Their Kajdar, the Kajdar that should have been theirs, had tragically died at the age of seven, years before Dany had met Fran. I remembered the train crash. I should have been in this train, but my family got directed to the wrong platform and missed it.

And there I was, bereft and reeling from yet another death. And here they were, itching to connect with me and join in a Triad. To learn how to develop their untapped powers. To teach the pupils of their school how to use and hone the abnormal abilities gifted to them by Mother Nature. The last hope for humanity.

CHILDREN OF THE SAND

Forty kids to escort from Port Central to BioDome One through a sandy desert inhabited by creatures including the occasional giant worm. And what looked like three suns. No wonder it's so hot.

Fortunately, the evenings were cool and the nocturnal cold temperatures bearable. Kids and soldiers wore desert scarves to protect their heads from heatstroke and their noses from the sand carried by the occasional violent gusts of wind. Soldiers wore goggles to protect their eyes. The kids refused the goggles. They had an extra transparent eyelid they can blink into place. Evolution.

The planet's velocity around its three suns was similar to Earth's. We were on the third planet from the Trappist-1 solar system in the Aquarius constellation, thirty-nine light years away from Earth.

The kids kept to themselves most of the time, whispering to each other in a language we didn't understand.

Every evening, Captain Sharid would follow the children's lead to establish camp. On the first evening, she ordered to halt. The children's faces were uncertain, and whispers travelled between them. At last, one of them stepped forward and said, "It is not safe here. A desert worm lives under this dune." A finger pointed in the direction of the dune.

Captain Sharid looked at the child thoughtfully for a long while before asking, "Where should we camp, then?"

The child looked around, checking their bearings. "This way. Twelve dunes away. It should be safe."

The camp would always be more extended than us soldiers thought needed. The children asked that we leave them some privacy for the exercise of natural bodily functions. Some of the soldiers laughed, but the Captain stared them down, and granted the children's request.

At night, us soldiers set up our tents in a loose circle at an acceptable distance from them. The children seemed to always find a desert tree to gather around.

On that first evening, a small group of them began busying themselves with something. I approached and saw a scorpion. I pointed my laser gun ready to obliterate the dangerous arachnid, but one of the children put her − or his − hand up.

"No! Let it be! It is not dangerous." The voice was as androgynous as the appearance. They were children of the desert and it was their planet. I guessed they knew better than I did.

The scorpion saw its window of opportunity and ran away. The children laughed and dispersed.

"Okay," I muttered, watching them. They had almost look-a-like appearances: copper-coloured skin from over-exposure to the suns, hair bleached by the harsh light falling short of their shoulders, like everyone we had seen on the planet so far.

The child who had spoken was still standing in front of me, her or his yellow-green eyes studying me. "I'm Keida." The face was serious, the accent as raspy as the sand and as edgy as a rocky mountain.

"I'm Corporal Rayan. You can call me Rayan." I smiled. But he, she… they… didn't smile back. The children never smiled at the soldiers. We were otherworlders.

We stood there for a minute and the child walked away. Boy or girl? I didn't know. Soldiers speculated about the kids' genders, but no one could figure it out. How old were they? The oldest maybe twelve or thirteen, the youngest five or six.

Every day we walked, the kids as hardy as the soldiers. Their garb was similar to what Tuareg people used to wear in the North-African desert of Earth before it became so hot and so arid that water totally evaporated in every oasis and no caravan could travel across it any more, and even lizards and snakes went sidelining elsewhere.

One evening, I found Private Pike lying on his front at the crest of a dune. He was too intent on his spying, eyes glued to his regulation binoculars, to notice my approach. I grabbed the back of his t-shirt, pulled him roughly and threw him to the sand. Pike was known for his dirty jokes, his dirty mind and his all-around dirty everything.

"Oi!" He rubbed the back of his shaved head. "What's your problem?"

I kicked the erection between his legs.

He screamed, his hands reaching to tenderly cradle the painful body part he was so proud of. He looked at me and grimaced. He suddenly unzipped his trousers and grabbed his swollen penis, showing it off. "Boy or girl, they could all do with some of that!"

I kicked the sand in front of me, hard. The sand flew to his exposed genitals. "Get yourself together, Pike. The Captain wants to see you. Now. And if I see you spying on the kids again, I promise you, you'll regret it with excruciating pain."

Anger distorting his face, he zipped up his trousers and carefully stood up. He picked up his binoculars and walked away, his legs wide apart to favour his painful manhood.

"Rayan."

I turned around. "Keida?"

"Is everything okay?"

"Yes, Keida, everything is okay." I couldn't help but wonder what Pike had seen through his binoculars, if anything at all.

Another child crested the dune. Thinner than Keida, but as tall.

"This is Bat," Keida told me. And to Bat, "This is Rayan. We're safe."

Bat nodded.

I walked back to the main camp. Like every unit, we were only ten soldiers, one corporal, one sergeant and one captain. While some disliked me, others respected me. Female soldiers knew I'd help them against the likes of Pike if they needed me to. Male soldiers knew to behave in my vicinity. We all wondered about the kids, but they had all learned to keep their dirty speculations to themselves in my presence. Except for Pike, of course, who had exacerbated even the most patient member of our unit, the captain herself. Pike was famous for having spewed smelly, acidic half-digested rations onto her boots after an evening of heavy drinking. He had spent forty-eight hours in the brig immediately after that. We were then only half-way between Earth and our destination…

Captain Sharid decided that Private Pike had to dig our latrines every evening. He hated it, one shovelling at a time. He hated it even more when he had to bury them in the morning. Some of his fellows had no qualms laughing at the inglorious duty. He blamed me.

* * * *

We stared at the ruins standing in front of us. BioDome One? This was not what we expected: stone walls eroded by the desert winds, a few trees still growing here and there, a broken well where a few lizards sunned themselves. And too small for the city we had imagined.

"Rayan." Captain Sharid turned her hazel eyes to me. "Get one of the kids here. The one who talks to you. Keida, is it?"

"Yes, Captain." I ran to the end of our column, staring at each serious child in turn. Suddenly Keida smiled at me. I also recognized Bat's gloomy expression standing next to... them. "Keida. Captain Sharid asked to see you."

"Of course. She wants to know where we're at."

We walked back at a brisk pace. When we reached the Captain, I could see fascination in Keida's eyes.

"What is this place? Is it BioDome One?" The Captain was frowning.

"No, it is Klibah, the Forgotten City. It was abandoned a long time ago. It was beautiful. I've seen pictures."

"What kind of people lived here?"

Keida shrugged their shoulders. "People." Their eyes scanned the landscape all around us. "We should camp here tonight. On this side of Klibah. There are desert worms on the other side."

Captain Sharid watched Keida walk off, then looked at me and sighed, "Kids... Okay. It's early, but never mind. We don't want to deal with these bloody worms more than necessary." Her eyes searched for someone and zeroed in on him. She hollered, "Sergeant McCloud!"

The skinny man with broad shoulders ran to her and smartly saluted. "Captain!"

Some of the kids were already checking out a tree and exploring some of the ruins. I noticed Pike walking to the broken well and swiftly grabbing one of the lizards by its tail. A small child approached and spoke to him. The tone was serious, the words in their language. Pike laughed his malevolent laugh. I joined them and noticed the lust in Pike's eyes.

"What's going on?"

The child simply pointed a finger at the lizard.

"What?" said Pike. "Lizard meat would be a change from the rations."

"For all you know, it could be poisonous."

He stopped smiling. "Spoilsport." He dropped the lizard and walked off, kicking sand with his boots.

The lizard ran off to find its friends. The child nodded to me, apparently satisfied, and ran off to find the other kids. Children of the sand and protectors of lizards? Or had they saved Pike's life? They were a mystery.

Us, Earthlings − new to the planet − had been asked to escort the children as a sign of good will and willingness towards a peaceful and respectful relationship with the natives. The commander in charge of our incursion to Trappist-1 had agreed.

There had been a nomadic people taking these children across the desert, but they had disappeared and now the kids were overdue north-east. Or so we had been told. It was something of an enigma. While the natives we had met seemed to have a primitive technology, they were highly cultured, and while we struggled with the grammatical structure of their language, they had no problems learning military English. Apparently, they had at least two dozen words for sand and twice more for wind. They were peaceful people, but there was a predatory hint in their eyes. The adults appeared different from the children. All the adults, even through without facial hair, seemed male. Where were the women? I don't think anyone got an answer, because the word would have spread like wild fire…

But back to the desert. Sand covered only a quarter of the planet, and water about half. The last quarter was green plains and green mountains, but we had only detected signs of human life in the deserts. Electronic interference got in the way of our scanning of the forests.

I was a soldier by choice. Not much else to do on the overcrowded planet Earth had become. When I heard about the first manned mission to Trappist-1, I volunteered. I had no family. I wasn't afraid of a few months in a cramped military spaceship. Some didn't survive. Some were still recovering. It was a wonder that Pike, as unbalanced as he was, seemed to do so well. I don't think anyone would have missed him. Except for his mother.

I noticed the walls of Klibah were darker than the traditional ochre structures at Port Central. The temperature during the day was still a record high. The kids didn't seem to mind. The night temperature was slightly cooler.

That evening, while a group of us were quietly staring at the camp fire after eating our rations, a sound jerked us back to reality.

The children were singing: the sweet voices of girls, or boys before puberty. It was haunting, spellbinding. We stared at each other in amazement. Even Pike's face softened. It was the first time we had heard them singing. Was it a special rite or a ceremony for the forgotten city of Klibah?

That night, I dreamed the people of Klibah were hardy, wiry, and as tall as Masai.

But I still couldn't figure out their gender. I was secretly as curious as every soldier. Was there such a notion as gender on the third planet of Trappist-1? They were used to our physical differences now, but at first their puzzlement had been obvious. It was not just that they got used to us, it was more a case of carelessly discarding the subject. It seemed to have no value and no interest for them. Strange people. We could barely comprehend their culture. They seem so peaceful, despite the predatory glare in the eyes of the adults at Port Central. And the children... They didn't seem to belong with them. Was it why we were asked to take them to BioDome One? Their skin tone was lighter, their features less sharp. Captain Sharid had a degree in anthropology, but she was careful to keep her observations and speculations to herself, and for the report she'd write later.

* * * *

BioDome One was of yellow and red ochres with a geodesic structure that shone in the midst of its traditional houses. A trump sounded from the closest minaret: a long, clear sound aimed at the sky.

Soon, a person wearing a white djellabah and a pale blue headscarf walked towards us. Captain Sharid greeted the dignitary.

First, they bowed at each other, keeping eye contact, as we had learned was the tradition. Keida ran to them and bowed their head, too. The dignitary spoke a long sentence with a chaotic accent. I think the first word meant 'welcome' and somewhere in the mix another word meant 'expected'. Another word might have been 'storm'.

Keida translated, "Welcome, people of the faraway sister planet. You have been expected. You arrive at a most extreme time to take shelter, as a storm is brewing in the north."

We looked to the north. The sky was a blue hardened by solar heat. Not a hint of cloud.

The dignitary smiled, their features as soft as the children's, and their eyes, full of curiosity, as green as the forests we were not allowed to visit. They spoke again.

Keida translated again, "The skies of BioDome One are always deceptive, but the air tells us everything we need to know. Please," the left arm extended towards the city. "Come and take shelter. We have some quarters ready for you. And the children,"

100

their smile widened, "are a wonder to lay eyes upon." Keida smiled.

Our caravan followed the dignitary in their footsteps. Sand started to dance in the air currents here and there as we reached the first houses. The streets were empty. I guessed the people were all in their houses. Windows were shuttered with planks of wood. Wood? Where were they getting this wood from?

The dignitary picked up their pace on the main street towards the geodesic dome. Its windows, too, were barred with wood. We followed our guide, taking a sharp left into a tall earth structure just before the street circling the central dome. We found ourselves in a wide room with wide steps carved in the rocky ground, leading deep underground. Two people waited at the foot of the stairs with torches that gave off an aroma of sweet oil and incense. The first sharp crack of thunder sounded as we entered a tunnel.

At the end, we stepped into a wide, round and natural room washed in wavering light from torches hung on the walls. It was completely empty. The dignitary gestured towards one of many openings: one with no shadow fluttering over its threshold. Keida, Bat and the other kids rushed for it, laughing and chatting. Keida stopped suddenly, walked back towards me and declared, "We will see you later. I'll be your mediator." ~~She~~ They flashed me a happy smile and ran after the other kids.

Mediator? The dignitary gestured towards another light-bathed opening. We slowly and cautiously crossed the threshold into a bare room, empty except for a natural pond in one corner: our guest quarters.

Like almost every other soldier there, my heart rose at the thought of finally being able to wash the dust and sweat from my skin. Almost every other soldier. Out of the corner of my eye, I caught Pike's mouth turn up in a smirk.

But before I could rebuke him, one of the female soldiers turned towards him. "One lusty look from you and I won't just erase it from your face, I will kill you with my bare hands."

Pike smirked and shrugged his shoulders as a reply.

"Quiet!" Captain Sharid said. "I expect each of you to behave. We all need a wash. We'll take turn."

* * * *

While the people of the third planet from the Trappist-1 system were willing to welcome newcomers, they were also cautious. I didn't blame them. Earth history was riddled with too much greed even if they knew nothing about it.

During our stay at BioDome One, we were not invited into the geodesic structure; I suspected due to technology that they weren't prepared to share with us. How else could they communicate with Port Central and other cities around the planet? But they didn't seem to care much for it. They were peaceful people. Quick learners, too, like the people of Port Central. And as much of a mystery.

As a mediator, Keida was present for every dealing with the dignitary. Keida was more than a mere translator; they would describe cultural differences in both languages. A facilitator, a communicator, a guide. I was impressed by their intelligence. Because they took me to many corners of the city, I got to witness many of their cultural quirkiness. As a consequence, I had many conversations with Captain Sharid to complement her anthropological report.

Still, the question remained. Were they intersex, or simply non-binary? Pike had no luck with any of the androgynous people he tried to have conversations with. Mostly, they just laughed at him.

102

The dignitary asked us to take another group of children with us for our return trip to Port Central.

They were different from Keida's group, and different again from the adults of BioDome One. They reminded us of the people at Port Central. What was the exchange about? Gifts to insure peace? They seemed to know nothing of war and its consequences.

When the Captain asked, the dignitary explained, "It has always been so. Our children flourish better with the climate of Port Central, and the children of Port Central flourish better in the climate here." Or something else they wouldn't share with us, despite Captain Sharid's subtle queries.

* * * *

We left BioDome One with as many questions as we had arrived with, and with a group of forty-two children who seemed to never smile.

I wore a pendant under my desert gear that had been made and gifted to me by Keida to remember them. It was a small, red semi-precious stone shaped like a lizard.

The trip back was uneventful, except for Private Pike falling foul of a desert worm under the feral eyes of forty-two quiet children. Since he didn't have any mother, no one missed him.

(edited by Jennifer L. Miller and previously published in the Ladies and Gentlemen of Horror 2014)

ALIVE OR DEAD

MICHAELA

THE BLOOD OF AN ENEMY

ALIVE OR DEAD

A first shot from my 7mm Remington Magnum digs a hole in his decomposing chest. His jeans are ragged and dirty. His hands, slowly propelled by arms decorated with remnants of tattoos, attempt to grab me. I fire a second shot and watch his head explode. Sloshy pieces of brain matter and sharp fragments of skull fly in every direction. He slowly collapses to his knees. This zombie came alone, but a rifle is noisy. I will not wait for unwanted company. Because I have no idea if an animal could turn into a zombie just by eating the decomposed remains, I spare a minute to sprinkle some gas out of a small can I looted from a convenience store, the kind used to recharge lighters, and drop a lit match. It is a hot summer morning, so I don't stand by the improvised pyre to watch the colourful flames dance joyfully. I walk away, reloading my rifle. Not a sign, not a sound of life. I wonder again if a zombie should be labelled 'alive' or 'dead', and once again my mind draws a blank. The word 'undead' is still a temporary fit.

The zombie plague began only two months ago, but this small town is already empty of human life. No one knows how it spreads. Despite the lack of intelligence of these undead, the governments and militaries were quickly overwhelmed by the situation. Probably because of human stupidity. At first, no one wanted to believe there were zombies. They thought this was a contagious disease spreading among the homeless; then theories started to abound. Extreme case of rabies. A mutation of the mad-cow disease. Radiations from outer space. Someone dug out a thesis on the ataxic neurodegenerative satiety deficiency syndrome (caused by an infectious agent) and uploaded it on the internet. But the favourite for the conspiracy theorists is, obviously, a secret, military bio-weapon gone wrong.

I guess I was one of the rare people noticing the difference. I happened to be obsessed with self-defence. Why? Why not. I used to do 50 press ups every morning, train at kung fu three times a week, run a few miles every evening, and shoot at my local fire range every Saturday. I was ready, and the weight of weapons is nothing for my muscles.

So, here I am, in a small town in the south, dispatching lone zombies. I haven't seen one survivor for a few days, not even a dog or a cat. I haven't even seen more than three zombies at a time. I wonder where they congregate in numbers. Maybe I should try a big city, if I get bored. I wipe sweat off my forehead and keep on walking on the cobbled street. I am not even looking for survivors; last time it was rather boring: humans can become so predictable with their delusions of self-importance. Thus, I walk alone, relying only on myself, the regular sounds of my boots echoing in the empty streets.

A shuffling behind me attracts my attention. I turn around at the same time as I pull the rifle out of my back harness. I'm already shooting the first zombie in the head. He was already missing an eye; my shot takes out the rest of his face and what passes for his brain. Next zombie is a fresh corpse that used to be female. Why shooting the head? If it is virus, the infection is likely to reside in the brain stem; but whatever it is, the brain controls motor functions. Severing the neck with a machete does the same trick if they come too close, and that's how I dispatch the fourth zombie after clubbing the third one with the butt of my rifle. I learned speed in my kung-fu training. While they are generally slow, a group of them can easily surround you. By the time the sixth and last corpse falls to the ground in a splatter of gore, it is too late for me. My guard has always been a bit weak, today it is fatal: my right arm now sports a zombie bite. It oozes blood and starts stinging. In the next few days, I'll find out if I am immune to the zombie plague, or not.

Another quick pyre later, I retire into a ravaged pharmacy and take a closer look at my arm. I'm lucky to find a sink with running water at the back. After watching water and blood mix together in the sink for a few minutes, I find a box of clean paper towels in a cupboard to dry my arm. I generously sprinkle the bite with various antiseptics left by the previous raiders. It stings. Foraging some more in the back of the shop, I find some penicillin and decide it'll have to do. I forage some more and find a few chocolate bars in a drawer. I stuff bandages, antiseptics, antibiotics and chocolate, into my rucksack. A pang of hunger lets me know it is lunchtime. I bite into a chocolate bar. My right forearm wrapped in a clean bandage, I gather my gear and leave the pharmacy. I head north, planning to leave this town, walking in the shade to avoid the blazing stare of the sun.

My arm hurts and the white bandage has dark red stains blossoming by the time I reach a supermarket at the edge of the town. I wipe sweat from my forehead and my neck. My forehead feels warm. I might have a touch of fever. I swallow some penicillin, prepare my Magnum and step through a broken glass wall, my eyes everywhere. You never know where the zombies will shuffle from. I hear there were zombies who could run. I could outrun them, if they really exist, but I do not wish to meet them. The shuffling zombie is bad enough, even with its lack of coordination and unsteady stride. Ever seen a group of zombies tripping over each other? Don't laugh, not even a chuckle, they're not deaf. They're slow, but they're dangerous in number. Expect them everywhere, behind you, but they're dangerous in number. Expect them everywhere, behind you, in front of you, above you, feasting on a freshly killed human being in what must have been the bakery section. Silently I retrace my steps. Where is the aisle for canned food? And now I've got an itch that I shouldn't scratch. As soon as possible I need to clean my wound again. The bandage is soaking dark and bloody.

Later I decide to find myself a deserted corner, far from the nearest church to avoid a gathering of zombies. I won't light a fire. While zombies haven't got eagle eyes, they seem to have a sixth sense to detect living humans. I don't want to make it easy for them. Leaving the road behind me, I walk towards a cluster of tall trees. The wide trunk and low branches of a mighty oak should provide me with a temporary shelter out of zombies' reach, but easy for me to climb to. It turns out to be difficult. My muscles feel weak. I make it to a branch high enough for safety, but with enough width to sit comfortably, my back leaning against the trunk. The foliage hides me from the ground. I am feeling hot and sweaty, and it is not just the weather. I undo the soaked bandage and look at the ugly wound. It is infected. I swallow some antibiotics and thoroughly clean my arm with antiseptic. It hurts like hell and I clench my teeth.

That night I sleep a fitful sleep with feverish dreams of zombies. I see the faces of my friends, their eyes haggard and dead, just before I shoot them. It was the first wave. They had been at the wrong place at the wrong time. I see their brains explode. Bloody grey splatters flying in every direction. I avoid hands and sever

110

some with my machete, along with a few heads and a few legs. They didn't want to believe it would happen. They laughed at me and my factual tales of zombies. They laughed at my regimen of regular exercises. I was right, but I am not laughing.

I wake up with dawn, shaking and sweating heavily. I dig in my rucksack for antibiotics. My movements feel like slow motion. I take a swig of water and my hand loosens its grip on the bottle. The bottle falls to the ground. My eyelids are so heavy; they fall over my eyes.

I dream again. My friends and their greyish features, no longer my friends, already dead and zombies. I have my back against a wall. I keep shooting them, but they keep coming back. When my Magnum clicks empty, I drop it and lift up my machete, deadly with it. But the zombies who used to be my friends keep coming back. No matter how many times I swing my machete, no matter how many heads roll, they keep coming back, grabbing at my clothes. A set of teeth bites my arm. The pain would make me scream. I open my eyes. The sun is high in the sky, almost in noon position, and my bitten forearm is swollen and throbbing.

The next time I open my eyes, I'm surrounded with darkness. The ground feels hard and cool. I wonder when I fell off the tree. It is quiet all around me. Keeping my eyes open is simply too difficult. I don't even try to move. Going back to sleep, returning to oblivion, feels so good.

I dream that I am crawling over the surface of the Earth.

I dream that I am climbing out of a ravine.

I dream that two zombies walk past me and ignore me.

When the sun rises again, I open my eyes. I feel tired, but I feel ok. I look around me. I am leaning against a wall at the end of a deserted road. How did I get into this town? I sense human presence nearby. I look around the corner and see two wimin armed with rifles. Life. I extend my arms in anticipation. Hunger slowly propels my shuffling feet forward.

MICHAELA

Jo remembered it as vividly as if it had happened that morning, with all the colourful details, including Michaela's ghostly grey shade in her eyes and the blazon on her sport jacket. She remembered the fullness of the moon high in the sapphire sky and the few trees shadowing the narrow passage. Her niece Patricia had barely known Michaela, being so young back then, but she remembered Jo's lover because Michaela had such a bright brand of smile that made her totally unforgettable.

Patricia was 15 now and, being perceptive, had known of the relationship between the two for a long time, and never had a problem with it. To have a problem with it would mean to be an obsolete, unnecessary, and useless bigot. As far as she was concerned Jo was the coolest sportswriter on the planet, and for Jo's sake, she wished that Michaela was still around.

As incredible as the story might sound, Patricia believed it as much as Jo did, even if, obviously, she had not witnessed it. She believed Jo, she was aware of Jo's sadness on the rare occurrences Michaela was mentioned, she knew that it was the source of her aunt's constant seriousness.

How had Michaela's name infiltrated itself in the conversation tonight? Patricia had no idea. But it had and, once again, she and her aunt were hypothesizing about the mysterious disappearance. At the time, Jo couldn't compete with Michaela anymore, but she was a staunch supporter. A skateboarding accident had deprived her of her favourite activity, what was going to be her career and her success. Michaela had been there every step of the way, reminding her that there was more to life than climbing and skateboarding. They had known each other since their early teen years, but it took Jo's fall for their love to blossom, for Jo to realize that words were as good a path to her as sport still was for Michaela. As much a prodigy as Jo had been, Michaela was, and had just signed her first sponsorship at the same time that Jo had started collecting academic degrees to propel herself into a new career. They had each other, they had it all. The world was their oyster…

Tonight Michaela was in their words again, out and loud and proud, and still so present in her absence. Outside the moon was conspicuous by her invisibility.

"We didn't believe it, we couldn't believe it, it was just superstition. 'Keep on the slabs if you must walk there at night, if you really must'. So we had been told……." Jo recalled out loud. St Mary's passage was narrow, barely wide enough for the three-foot-wide slabs and some dirt that grew a few skeletal trees every now and then. It would take brave – or stupid – people to walk from the market place where griffins spat water away from the fountain (or so Jo and Michaela had claimed as long as they had known each other) to the graveyard that surrounded the church dedicated to St Mary.

"When I was a child, I thought churches were roman and cathedrals were gothic, always." Jo kept reminiscing for Patricia's benefit. St Mary's church was gothic. Back in the 17th century soldiers fallen during the Civil War had been buried upright, including under St Mary's passage, since there were so many of them, and so little space left around the church. Elders told them about the low moaning of the dead (they had dismissed it as leaves rustling in the wind), warned them about the hands of the dead reaching up through the cracks between the slabs and grabbing at ankles, pulling people down into the underground for all eternity. Jo remembered out loud again, "In the chill of the night I kept to

114

the slabs. Michaela didn't. I saw the skinny fingers grab at her trouser legs. She shrieked. She called out my name for help. She was 30 feet ahead of me. I ran as fast as I could with my bad leg. I threw the bottom end of my walking stick for her to grab. Her legs had already disappeared underground. Her hands slid down my stick. I saw her being pulled between the slabs, within a crack, in slow motion..."

Michaela hated the feel of their cold, skinny fingers poking, grabbing, probing all over her body, violating her skin. But once she was lowered down to their feet, they forgot about her and ignored her. When she tried to stand up and reach up to the cracks she could just guess in the darkness a few feet above their heads, their hands were all over her again. So she stayed down. She guessed it was daytime when they didn't move. She didn't feel like moving either, letting her eyelids weigh heavily over her eyes. She felt the night through the current of agitation passing through them, their hungry fingers reaching up for the slabs, but passers-by were rare and avoided the cracks, they knew. She felt no thirst, no hunger, no physical needs. She wanted out, but couldn't guess the exit. She knew osmosis would eventually turn her into one of them, so she hung onto her love, the memory of her love...

Michaela daydreamed of the love she had lost by foolishly stepping on a crack. She ran it through her mind over and over again. When she slowed down her daydreaming, the empty sleeplessness of the dead soldiers would sneak into her consciousness, invading it thought by thought, like fingers prodding and probing. She felt like screaming, but couldn't find her voice. She wanted to call out her love's name and break out of this dead swamp that wanted to swallow her. Her love's name would bring light to her mind every time and push away the intrusive fingers.

Her breathing would slow down, her heartbeat would calm down. Was she still breathing? Was her heart still beating? Was she still alive? Or had the army of dead soldiers already made her one of them and her mind itself was a delusion?

So Michaela kept on repeating her love's name like a mantra. She kept on visualising her love's face like a mandala. Unaware of the passing of time. If you have no landmark, is there such a thing as time? There, underground, the dead were timeless, and so was Michaela.

Jo took a deep breath, her eyes on the trio of framed, A4 photos lined on the wall above the silent mantelpiece. On the left, Michaela doing a kick flip in their favourite skate park. On the right, Jo doing a matching kick flip (on the day she drastically injured herself). In the middle, Jo and Michaela smiling and holding hands. The three photos had been taken by Jo's sister, Patricia's mother, who had always been a friend, as much as a sister to Jo. She closed her eyes, exhaling a long breath. It had been ten years, but Jo refused to forget, refused to close the door to a past she wanted to be still present.

An odd noise broke the spell. It sounded like a loud and desperate scratching against the wooden front door. Was it real or a figment of imagination? Jo and Patricia looked at each other. They heard it a second time.

The only sounds the dead ever made were from the rough fabric of their tattered army clothing rubbing against other uniforms, and from their dirty cracking boots shuffling on the ground. She couldn't see their features; she could barely guess their silhouettes in the dark. In her mind's eye they looked like zombies, but she knew they were not. They were mute.

    Michaela learned that if she simply crawled on the uneven floor of this world of the dead, the dead would ignore her. So she crawled, scratching her hands and tearing her clothes on the occasional sharp stones pointing out of the dirt, feeling no pain in this strange world, feeling no desire, but still feeling stubborn. Her love was waiting for her; she was sure of it. Her love was calling for her; she could hear her voice in her mind's ear. Her love was all over her mind, carrying her, pushing her, pulling her. And Michaela crawled and crawled between the feet of the dead, timelessly and endlessly, breathlessly. But was she still breathing? Was she still alive? She didn't know anymore, but she crawled...

Jo grabbed her walking stick and got up from her armchair, "I'm going to check on this commotion," she said, waving at Patricia to stay put. She limped her way to the corridor, her footsteps resonating on the wooden floor. The front door squeaked when she opened it. A body tumbled into her, pressing her against the wall for balance. This body felt barely alive, barely conscious. This body was covered with an uneven coat of dirt and mud. The torn clothes might once have been a sport suit. Jo called out to Patricia for help. Her bad leg was too weak to keep up in a standing position under this double weight.

    Patricia arrived just in time to catch them and ease them down to the floor. The newcomer was unconscious behind her closed eyelids, under the curtain of dirty, colourless hair. The body felt thin, almost skinny, almost weightless. The eyelids fluttered and slowly rose up; Jo stared into the faded light of grey eyes. A skeletal hand reached out to her arm and remained there, motionless.

Michaela crawled and crawled, her fingers digging the dirt, holding on to the eyes her love's name evoked, seeing them in the perpetual darkness surrounding the soldiers. She crawled and dug, until she dug herself out of a gutter. The lights of the deserted night blinded her and she closed her eyes, hanging on to the sound of her mantra. The sound of this simple syllable, "Jo," was like a siren pulling her forward along the hard ground. She kept on crawling, the eyes of her love like a beacon in her mind's eyes. Mindlessly she went on, unaware of her surroundings, animal instinct guiding her, dragging her on.

Her head gently bumped into a wooden door. She willed her hands to the door, willed herself upright, the mantra singing inside her. She pushed her fingers along the solid wood; her fingers had stopped bleeding a long time ago, but they kept the scratching motion going. She scratched and pushed until the door gave in and she fell into a warm body, blinded by dim electric light. She felt eased down to the floor, strangely comfortable in her love's warm arms. It could only be her love. She slowly relaxed into the strong embrace. She opened her grey eyes to the warmth of hazel irises and reached out a hand up to one of the reliable arms holding her. She had no words left. She had escaped the intrusive fingers of the dead soldiers. She smiled and closed her eyes for the last time.

THE BLOOD OF AN ENEMY

"Tiger, they found Cicely wandering on the road, regularly running back to the burning cars, and howling by the driving door of your car."

"I let her out of the car."

"But you were dead. You were still at the wheel of your car. You died instantly when the other car crashed into yours."

"I don't know how I did it. I just know I did. Dogs trust their humans with their lives. The engine of the other car was about to explode. I couldn't let her die."

"But you were dead!"

"I know. I know I was already dead."

Rikki wakes up and rolls on to her left side. In the grey light of dawn, Cicely lifts her head up and wags her tail.

* * * *

Rikki is running barefoot in the sand with her husky Cicely. It is their morning routine. Two miles from the lighthouse she bought last year as a secret hideout with her now dead lover, to the coffee shop and B&B run by her childhood friend Anna in St Hilda. She is wearing her usual seaweed green t-shirt and cargo shorts, one side pocket bulging with a thick notebook. Cicely has black markings around the eyes that give her an evil look, denied by goofy behaviour. By the time they reach the Rainbow Cove, it is barely 8 am. She sits at her usual table and opens the local news rag laying there. Soon Anna is bringing her a cappuccino and sitting with her.

She ruffles Rikki's short and curly hair. Cicely has already drunk part of the water that was waiting for her under the table. There is now a puddle around the dog's bowl. The husky rests her head on the woman's lap. Anna's hair is blonder than Rikki's and definitely longer. "Morning, sunshine! How is business?" Rikki's blue eyes meet Anna's green, but don't return the smile.

"An acceptable number of words, enough inspiration to resume writing later. What about yours?"

Anna grimaces, "Suddenly booming. Today will be busier than yesterday. Holiday people are ALL arriving tomorrow." Anna strokes the head of the quiet husky. "How are you doing?" Rikki looks away. Silence settles. The last cirrus clouds disintegrate in the sky. "How is Cicely?"

"Fifty-fifty."

"In your own time, my friend, in your own time." Rikki's eyes are fixated on the mesmerizing sea. "So, what is now happening in your writing world?"

The blue eyes meet the green ones again. "I'm considering aliens."

"In a fantasy novel?"

"It is speculative fiction."

"Of course," Anna smiles. Rikki's facial features relax. Anna gently pushes the husky's head off her lap and gets up. "Gotta drive to town now. Amber will bring you breakfast."

"Amber? What happened to Helen?"

"Helen cancelled due to a family emergency. Amber was the next available option."

"Ah."

Anna squeezes Rikki's shoulder. "See you tomorrow."

"Have a good day." Rikki gets the small notepad and a pen out of her side pocket while Anna walks away and Cicely lies down on the cool concrete ground of the terrace. Rikki starts writing and drinking her cappuccino slowly and distractedly.

The Tetralians were from another galaxy. The few thousands travelling through space in a dozen spaceships were the last of their species. Their food supplies were getting too low even for rationed comfort when they happened upon a planet with several landmasses and mostly water. They noticed creatures of various species living in harmony with their environment. They noticed creatures with peelable skins destroying the living beings and green foliage and clawing the rich soil to build clusters of monstrosities to live in. They didn't seem to be particularly nice to each other, or maybe it was part of their tradition and culture to hit each other as a form of greeting.

Each Tetralian vessel sent a party of a hundred or so hunters to attack some of the middle-sized clusters at dawn. They shot to kill. Within an hour they had killed enough of these creatures to feed themselves while searching the universe for a suitable planet to colonize–

"Vegeburger and fried eggs?"

A young womon is standing by her table, carrying a tray. The husky sits up. Rikki's eyes look up from her notes and study the smiling features. She notices the make-up, the low-cut top revealing a cleavage, the long wavy hair, the legs not yet tanned.

"Yes," Rikki doesn't smile back.

Amber moves the plates to the table, pretends to just notice the notebook. "Oh, you're a writer or something?"

Rikki frowns and pointedly closes her notebook. Cicely's ears perk up, suddenly alert. "Or something."

"A reporter then?" Amber's smile broadens.

"I'm here for breakfast." Rikki's body tenses up. A low growl escapes from Cicely.

"Oh. Holler if you need something!" Amber walks away, her hips swaying to the rhythm of her footsteps, Rikki's stare following her. By the time Amber looks back just before entering the kitchen, Rikki has already refocused on her notebook.

* * * *

Every morning Rikki and Cicely run to the Rainbow Cove for breakfast. After a brief chitchat with Anna, she writes in her notebook and drinks a cappuccino while Cicely lazes under the table. After a while, Amber brings her fried eggs and a vegeburger, and tries to engage her into conversation. On the fourth morning, the beaming Amber sits at the table and tells Rikki, "I know who you are; you are Richelle Fox; you wrote Tiger Vox's authorized biography."

Rikki stares at the waitress, but doesn't smile. "Who I am is irrelevant, especially when I'm on holiday."

"It's ok. It's a great book actually." Amber keeps on smiling, still sitting across the table. Cicely, sensing Rikki's tension, sits up and starts growling.

"My dog doesn't like you. I strongly advise you go back to the kitchen."

With her irritating smile still plastered across her face, Amber stands up. "Enjoy your breakfast!" Forever swaying her hips for Rikki's benefit, she walks away confidently, unaware that Rikki is not even looking at her. Stroking Cicely's head soothingly, she contemplates the peaceful ocean and sighs slowly.

Later, Anna sits on the chair vacated by Amber. She smiles and teases, "I think Amber fancies you."

Rikki stretches while the husky reaches for Anna's hand with her head. After a thoughtful moment, Rikki replies, "She is a nosey parker. Are you sure she is just a waitress?"

Anna's smile slowly fades. She frowns. "What do you mean?"

"She asks a lot of questions. And she just asked me if I were Richelle Fox."

Anna recovers her smile. "So what? Maybe she is a fan?"

"My publisher hasn't released any photos of me and I don't do the book-signing thing."

"But it is no secret that you followed Tiger Vox on tour to write the biography."

Rikki rubs the bridge of her nose. "I know. But I am here on holiday. I'm here for healing. I'm here for........"

"To forget?"

"I could never forget her." Anna squeezes her friend's hand. Cicely moves to Rikki and lays her head on the writer's lap. "I want my privacy to be respected. I want to .... grieve in my own time."

"Ok. From now on, I'll bring your breakfast myself."

Rikki's eyes move back to the ocean, but she doesn't see the gentle waves sparkling under the sun. She sees Tiger Vox in her resplendent drag king persona: short dark hair, challenging stare, smoky suit and red tie. As she appeared on the cover of her first album, 'Queer Boi'. She remembers it well. A statement, a pamphlet. A modern rock sound with a metal edge and goth moments. A voice with bluesy echoes rumbling and reaching deep inside. And lyrics twisting your mind, knifing your heart, and taking you to the other side of the universe. She had taken the country by surprise, and by storm. She looked so perfectly androgynous with her square jaw and her unplucked eyebrows. She was bold and intelligent, witty and spiritual, and an uncompromising atheist. She was rock and roll.

"I'll see you tomorrow!" Anna brings her back to the ocean and the summer. "I think today's gonna be a scorcher!"

"Yes, looks like it. See you tomorrow."

* * * *

And every night Rikki dreams. She is standing at the foot of the lighthouse, bathing in the moonlight, twenty feet above the sea. Tiger Vox is there, too, and Cecily is happy. And they talk. They talk about the car crash (it was not a hate crime, it was really an accident); they talk about the novel Rikki is currently writing; they talk about life and death. But Tiger is an immaterial spirit and they cannot touch each other.

One night, sitting on the rocks and admiring the waves, Tiger Vox says, "There is a way." Her voice has a serious quality.

"What way?"

Tiger sighs. "An unsuitable way."

One of Rikki's eyebrows rises. "How unsuitable?"

"A human sacrifice in the early hours of Lammas." Silence ensues. They both stare at the dark waves under the starry sky.

"Lammas," Rikki eventually muses aloud. "An Anglo-Saxon festival marking the first harvest of the year. Generally on the first day of August."

"There was a custom. The first loaf of bread made with the new crop was blessed in church. Then it could be used for magic." The gender-queer ghost chuckles softly. "One book of charms advises to break the blessed loaf into four pieces and place a piece in each corner of the barn, to protect the newly harvested grain."

"You mentioned a human sacrifice......."

"On the same date, there is Lughnasadh." She is quiet for a minute, listening to the waves crashing below and beating the rocks. "Irish Gaelic. About harvest, too. A feast commemorating the sacrifice of a Celtic god. Lugh, god of light and son of the sun."

"Were the Celts literal?"

124

The musician smiles at her lover and shrugs. "I don't know. I wasn't there! According to mythology this god would transfer his power to the grain and was sacrificed when this grain was harvested."

"The Wicker Man, isn't it from the same tradition?"

Tiger laughs heartily. "It's a music festival in Scotland! Good crowd. A few days before Lammas, actually. Similar roots, I guess."

"There is a movie."

"Yes, there is, but this is not what I'm talking about." Her facial features turn serious again. "The spirits whisper." Her voice quietens and is now barely above a whisper. "If the blood of an enemy is spilled near a portal. On the shore. In the early hours of Lughnasadh. The portal will open and the desired spirit will be able to cross over and take solid form." She lowers her head. Her immaterial hand strokes the husky. Cecily's eyes meet hers. The dog smiles, feeling a shiver across her fur where the spirit's hand has touched her.

The writer takes a deep breath and murmurs, "The blood of an enemy......."

* * * *

Anna steps into the room. She has sent Amber on an errand to the local supermarket. She looks at the room. Thirty minutes is all she's got to search through Amber's mess. A pile of underwears grace the floor next to the unmade bed. The chest of drawers is bursting with clothes and covered with various items, including an abundance of make-up and a laptop. Anna thinks that the laptop is probably password-protected. A handbag is keeping company with a pair of sandals behind the door. She has convinced Amber to leave immediately, placating her with the keys to her van.

Anna kneels down to the floor and her hands dive into the big leather handbag. She finds a compact mirror, a pen, a phone (password protected), a few cards and a notebook. One of the cards is a press card issued to Amber Logan. She skims the pages of the notebook, looks through a list of names and recognizes some.

"Rainbow Cove, St Hilda

Richelle Fox aka Jill Silkies?"

She wonders where she's seen the name of Jill Silkies. Something to do with books. She can't remember exactly. If Jill Silkies is a writer, Anna hasn't read any of her works. She wonders what could be the association with Rikki. Her friend writes fantasy or speculative fiction with the occasional non-fiction. She sighs. Maybe Rikki is right; Amber is a reporter. But what would she want from Richelle Fox? Anna leaves Amber's room and walks to her office where she switches her computer on. Her PC hums to life and soon she is searching the net for Jill Silkies. The writer is easy to find. Within the last five years she has published five lesbian erotic novels that have quickly become popular.

Anna whistles quietly. She looks out the window to the sea shining under the sun, trying to connect the details together.

Amber steps into the room at the same time the computer sighs out and off. She hands over a pack of printing paper, the keys to the van, a receipt and some change.

"Thanks, Amber. Tell me something."

"Yes?" Amber smiles her usual confident smile, bright and inviting.

"What are you doing here?"

Amber's smile fades a notch and turns to guarded. "What do you mean?"

"You're a reporter. What are you looking for?"

126

"What?"

"Don't deny it."

"Well, it's hard to make a living as a reporter. I sometimes have to do other jobs."

"Blah dih blah. I want the truth, Amber. Why are you after my friend Rikki? What do you want from her?"

Amber chuckles. "You're very protective of her, aren't you."

Anna just stares.

Amber sighs. "Ok. I know she is the writer Richelle Fox, the author of Tiger Vox's authorized biography. I'm working on an article about her."

"I don't buy it, Amber. Tell me the REAL truth."

"Ok. Ever read any books by Jill Silkies?"

"Nope."

"Well, Jill Silkies has written some extremely popular lesbian erotic novels. She is a big name."

"So?" Anna shrugs. "No connection with Richelle Fox."

Amber chuckles again. "She is your friend and she hasn't told you...... Richelle Fox is Jill Silkies. How does it feel to have such a good friend keeping secrets from you?"

Anna's facial expression doesn't vary. "What have you got to back up your claim?"

Amber's voice becomes excited, "How do you think she could afford her lighthouse? She bought it before the publication of Tiger Vox's biography. My sources are always solid. That's how I found out that Jill Silkies eats breakfast at the Rainbow Cove every morning. Richelle Fox is the only writer around here."

"No one knows who Jill Silkies is. Thus, anyone in St Hilda could be Jill Silkies, including me."

"No. Richelle Fox is Jill Silkies. My instinct never fails me."

Anna shakes her heard. "You're fired."

Amber laughs. "You can't fire me! The B&B is too busy at the moment; you couldn't run it on your own. Besides, by law, you would have to give me a week's notice."

"Here you go, consider yourself notified. I want you gone when your week is up."

The two wimin stare at each other. Humour is conspicuous by its absence.

* * * *

It is after midnight and Rikki is sitting at the foot of the lighthouse, Cicely's head resting on her lap. Their moods harmonize in a mournful key, listening to the rhythm of the waves breaking on the rocks below. Their eyes stare at the slight haze floating in the shape of a doorway twelve feet away from them. *The blood of an enemy.* As a writer, Rikki kills frequently, on paper. She has killed many irritating people that way. The blood spilled is virtual, thus unsuitable for *the unsuitable way* her dead lover mentioned to her.

Suddenly Cicely lifts her heard, sniffs the night air and growls, jumping on her paws. Rikki looks around and stands up when she sees the irritating waitress from the Rainbow Cove walking towards her, her arrogant smile spread over her features.

"Hello! I'd love to have a chat with you!"

"And I would not."

"It's in your interest. I know who you are."

"My identity is not a secret."

"I am talking about—" A louder growl from Cicely interrupts her. She stops her advance and looks at the dog.

"Go away. You are not welcome here."

"I am about to reveal your secret identity to the world. I'm sure you'd rather it be in your own words."

"I don't know what you're talking about. Go."

128

"Come on! I know you are Jill Silkies." Amber's face suddenly looks shocked as she now stares beyond Rikki. "What's the hell is that?"

Rikki turns around and looks at the hazy colours floating in the air. They are increasingly vivid.

In her shock and amazement at the paranormal phenomenon, the reporter steps forward. Her advance is met by a snarling Cicely. Reflexively Amber steps back. And stumbles backward. She waves her arms in a useless attempt at recovering her balance, and screams as she falls towards the sea, bouncing on the rocks, breaking her bones and spilling her blood.

Rikki has rushed to the edge. She silently watches a rushing wave stealing the body away from the sharp rocks. *The blood of an enemy.* She slowly turns around and watches the vivid haze of the portal taking firmer shape. She can now distinguish the musician's silhouette. Soon she can guess the features and see the surprised smile. Tiger Vox is about to cross over the threshold. She opens her mouth to express disbelief, not sure if she should feel happy or sad. The blood of an enemy must have been spilled. Her right hand is taking hold of the portal frame when a dark shape brutally shoves her aside and fully crosses the portal, with a cavernous laughter resonating in the night. It looks smoking and red hot, seven or eight feet tall, with cruelty plastered over distorted facial features.

Cicely is the first one to react. She's lost one human already, she is not about to lose another one. She swiftly jumps at the creature, her jaws grab the throat and her fangs sink deep into the vulnerable flesh. The demon falls backward, dark blood spilling abundantly from its torn throat, before Rikki's amazed eyes.

Tiger Vox appears in the portal again. Rikki forgets about the thrashing demon who can't get rid of the stubborn, growling husky. This time, the musician crosses over. The two lovers embrace. The spirit, now solid, murmurs, "I haven't got much time."

* * * *

"You're late," says Anna, smiling, when the writer and the dog appear at the Rainbow Cove on the last stroke of 9 am. Rikki smiles back. She hasn't slept much, but she is feeling good. Anna notices the relaxed features. "I'll get your cappuccino right now." Walking to the kitchen, she thinks, "Even Cicely looks better."

REMEMBERING JENNIFER L.MILLER

February 13, 1978 – March 31, 2019

I wish I could say that we met while fighting hordes of demons and zombies. Or in a lost and deserted citadel on a faraway planet, only accessible via a portal opening only once every 100 years in the Four Corners reservation. Possibly when time travelling in an alternate Victorian 19th century where steampunk was the norm.

We actually met in cyberspace. Once upon a time there was a popular social website by the name of MySpace, where I tracked down the amazing writer and artist Jane Timm Baxter – now a spirit flying free, too. On Hallow's Eve 2008, Jane gave me a glimpse of the Ladies and Gentlemen of Horror, brain-child of the wonderful Jennifer L. Miller. To obtain a key to this extraordinary world fraught with demons, catastrophes and hope, I befriended Jenna. The rest is… a writer's tale.

In this world of darkness and abyss, Jenna was the guide with the keys and clues to make our words ring true in our quest for light. She was the forger of alliances, the oracle of forbiddings, the matchmaker from hell, the girl next door. Essentially, she was a friend.

REMEMBERING JANE TIMM BAXTER

April 16, 1976 – April 12, 2019

When Death came for you
You smiled
And said
"Yes, I'll gladly follow you"
And you trusted
That your dogs
Your husband, your friends
And your chosen family
Would understand

That Life – the bitch –
Had dealt you so much pain
Pain that painkillers
Wouldn't kill
All your husband could do
Was to sit down with you
Hold your hand
And wait
For the tsunami to pass

Will you still be
Proud of me
Will you still like
Everything I do
While I travel the river
To its elusive source
Following my own rhythm
And singing my own tune
Because it's all I know

May your spirit fly free
And soar high
My friend
You are loved
And forever remembered

ABOUT THE AUTHOR

W. Freedreamer Tinkanesh has self-published:

a novel, OUTSIDER, in spring 2012
and a collection of short stories, TALES FOR THE 21st
CENTURY volume 1, in spring 2014.

In the 21st century, W has contributed short stories to various
anthologies:

WRITE NOW (2002) *out of print*
THREADS (2009) *out of print*
ECLECTICA, The World of Shadows, a book of strange stories,
bizarre tales and otherworldly events (2011) *out of print*
OUT IS THE WORD by The Word Is Out (2012)
NO ONE MAKES IT OUT ALIVE, An End of the World
anthology (2012)
BLESSINGS FROM THE DARKNESS (2014)
THE LADIES AND GENTLEMEN OF HORROR 2014
THE LADIES AND GENTLEMEN OF HORROR 2017
ANOTHER PLACE (2018)

They also had poems in two anthologies:

POETS KNOW IT volume two (2002)
AN ANTHOLOGY OF BRIXTON POETS (2003/04)

Under the pseudonym River Wolf, they contributed to:
THE LADIES AND GENTLEMEN OF FANTASY 2014

Most of these books are available on amazon.

You can find W. Freedreamer Tinkanesh on Goodreads, Twitter and Facebook.

Printed in Poland
by Amazon Fulfillment
Poland Sp. z o.o., Wrocław